An Anthology of Small Adventures in a Big and Dangerous World

inquiry@ironcircus.com www.ironcircus.com

strange and amazing

MANAGING EDITOR
Amanda Lafrenais

COVER ARTIST
John Keogh

BOOK DESIGN
Matt Sheridan

PROOFREADER
Blue Delliquanti

first printing: December 2017 printed in Canada ISBN: 978-1-945820-12-

A PIG BEING LOWERED INTO HELL IN A BUCKET
KC Green

WHAT'S HAPPENING!
WHAT'S HAPPENING! WHAT'S HAPPENING! WHAT'S HAPPENING!
WHERE AM I!
AAAAAA

AH, OH WHERE AM I!
WHAT IS THIS NIGHT-MARE!
HELL
HELL
HELL
TO HELL! TO HELL!
I DIDN'T DO ANYTHING! I DIDN'T DO ANYTHING!!!
HELL
OH BOO HOO HOO!!
HELL! OH HELL!
WHAT DID I DO TO DESERVE THIS!
WHAT DID I DO!!
OH, YOU JUST... DIED!
THAT'S ALL IT TAKES, SOMETIMES!

DEAD?!
YEP, THAT'S THE AFTERLIFE FOR YA! THE FARMER TAKES CARE OF YOU ONLY TO USE OUR BODIES FOR HIS OWN PROFIT! BUHGAWK!
JUST TRYING TO LIVE BY EATING A FEW CHICKENS ...
...IS ENOUGH TO GET A FREE SHOTGUN BLAST IN ME CHEST!
WHAT'S NEW!!!
FOR FOXES!!
I BROKE MY LEG...
COLONY COLLAPSE!
ATED BY A BEAR!
I...
I DON'T KNOW WHAT HAPPENED...
I... I GOT SO MAD.. I DON'T UNDERSTAND HOW OR WHY BUT THE ANGER WAS REAL...
IT WAS THERE...

AND JANEY...
I LOVED HER I WOULD HAVE NEVER HAD DONE THAT NOT IN A MILLION, HUNDRED....
BUT I WAS SO MAD.
SOMETHING BIT ME AND I COULDN'T STOP...
THE ANGER WAS SO ... HOT.
AND... JANEY.... OH MY GOD!
MY GOD!
GOD, GOD! YES! HIM!
I WANNA TALK TO GOD,
I WANNA TALK TO GOD,
I WANNA TALK TO GOD,
I WANNA TALK TO GOD,
THIS IS ALLLL JUST A BIG MISUNDERSTANDING, AND I'D LIKE TO GO TO... THE
WHICH ONE IS THE GOOD PLACE
WHICH ONE IS THE ONE WHERE WE'RE NOT GOING TO.
LIKE HELL, BUT THE OTHER ONE
HHHHHH
HHHELL...2.
IS IT HELL 2?

I'D LIKE OPTION NUMBER TWO, PLEASE!!
THERE IS NO OTHER OPTION FOR ANIMALS!

WE HAVE NO SOULS IN THE EYES OF GOD. WE DON'T GET A CHOICE.

WHAT GOOD CAN ANY OF US DO WHEN, ULTIMATELY, WE STILL GET PUNISHED?

WHAT DOES IT MEAN TO TRY AND BE RIGHTEOUS IN HIS EYES,
WHEN GOD DOESN'T EVEN SEE US AS ANYTHING MORE THAN FOOD OR TOOLS.

NO, ALL WE ARE ARE PARABLES AND MAKE-BELIEVE THANKS TO THOSE JERKS.

THE BIBLE VILIFIES THE SNAKE. ALL OF WOMEN GET THE BLAME,

BUT NO ONE THINKS TWICE ABOUT THE APPLE.

WHY DOESN'T THE APPLE GET ANY KIND OF BAD RAP?

IT KEEPS THE DOCTORS AWAY!
SHUT UP!!!

SORRREEEEEE
JEEZ

NO,
WE GOT SCREWED.

WE WERE ACCEPTED BY OUR LORD AND DAMNED IN THE SAME BREATH.

THERE'S NOTHING ANYONE WHO GIVES A DAMN CAN DO.
THEY'RE NOT LISTENING...

IF WE ARE SO UNWORTHY, THEN WHAT I AM FEELING NOW?

IT'S...
IT'S A FEELING OF A WANT TO...
NOT BE UNWORTHY.

A DESIRE TO UNDER-STAND...
HOW TO BE OF WORTH.

IF WHAT I AM FOR HUMANS IS WORTH SOME-THING TO THEM,

DOES THAT NOT MAKE ME ONE OF WORTH ENOUGH TO NOT BE PUNISHED FOR IT?

HALT!

OO-

...

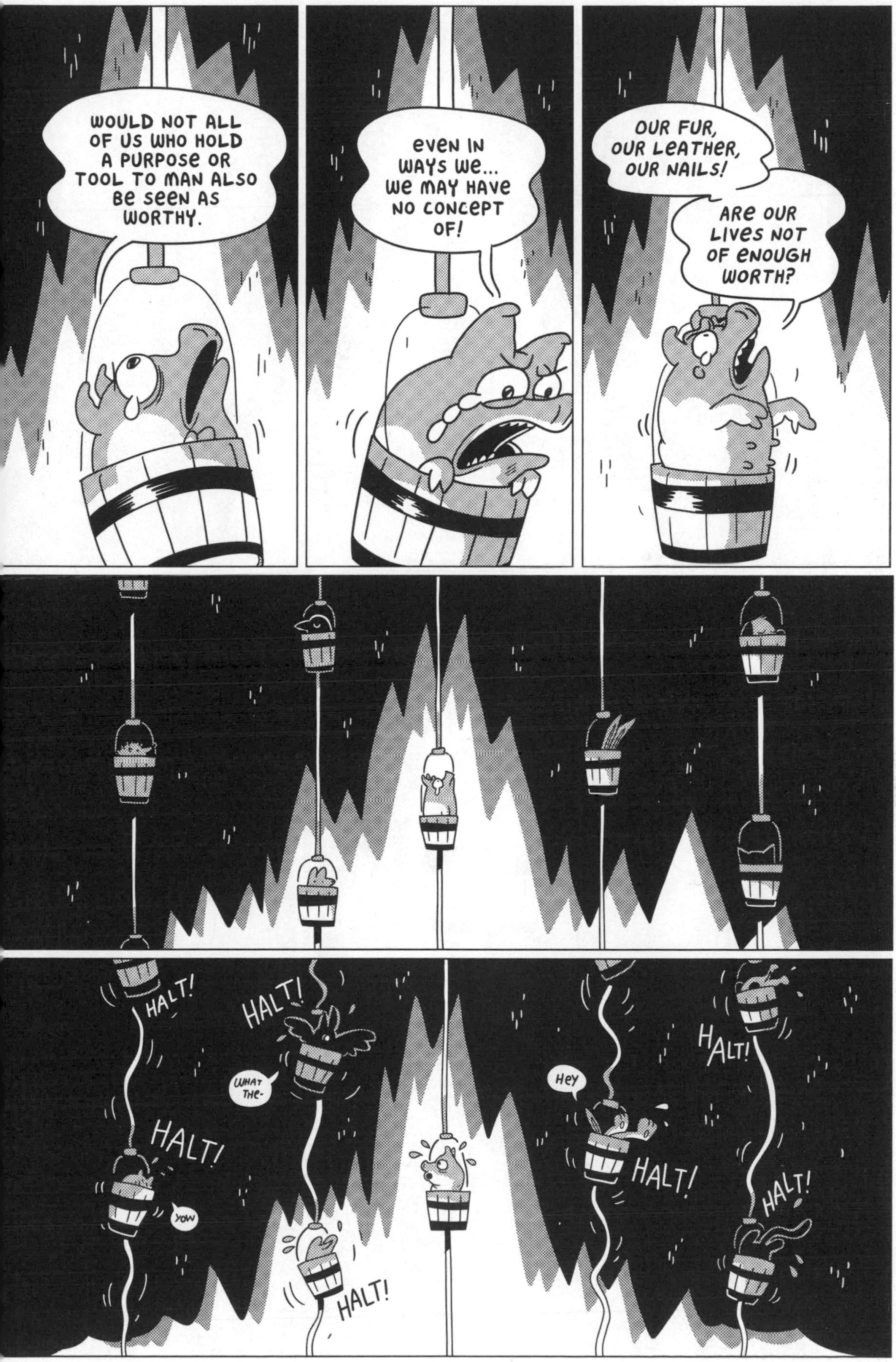

WOULD NOT ALL OF US WHO HOLD A PURPOSE OR TOOL TO MAN ALSO BE SEEN AS WORTHY.
EVEN IN WAYS WE... WE MAY HAVE NO CONCEPT OF!
OUR FUR, OUR LEATHER, OUR NAILS!
ARE OUR LIVES NOT OF ENOUGH WORTH?
HALT!
HALT!
WHAT THE-
HALT!
YOW
HALT!
HEY
HALT!
HALT!
HALT!

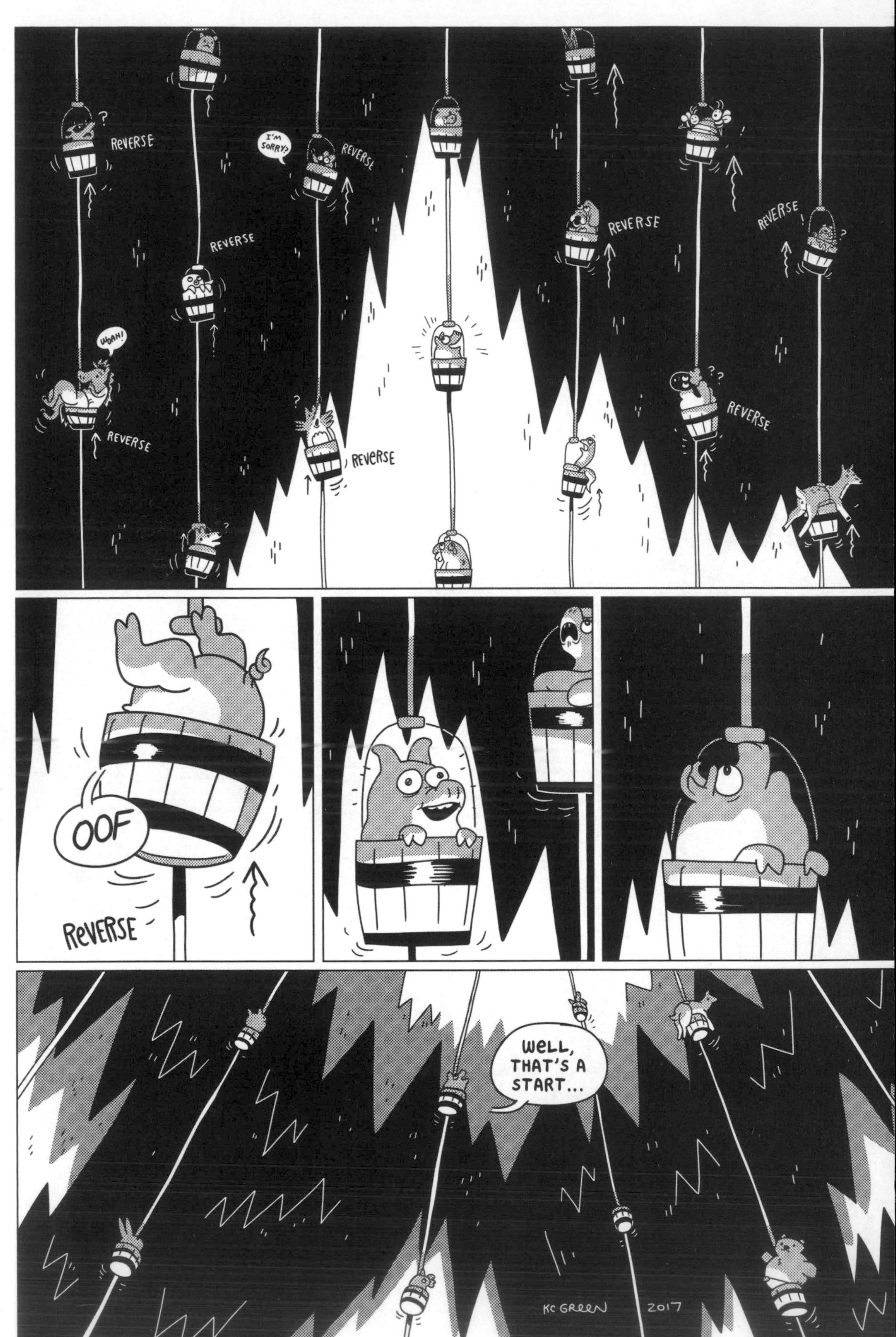
REVERSE
I'M SORRY?
REVERSE
REVERSE
REVERSE
REVERSE
WOAH!
REVERSE
REVERSE
REVERSE
REVERSE
OOF
REVERSE
WELL, THAT'S A START...
KC GREEN 2017

BETTER NATURE
Jemma Salume
PAFF
HAH! UNH!

WHERE... THIS ISN'T... WAS THE... WINDOW OPEN?
HM.
WHAT'RE YOU DOING HERE?

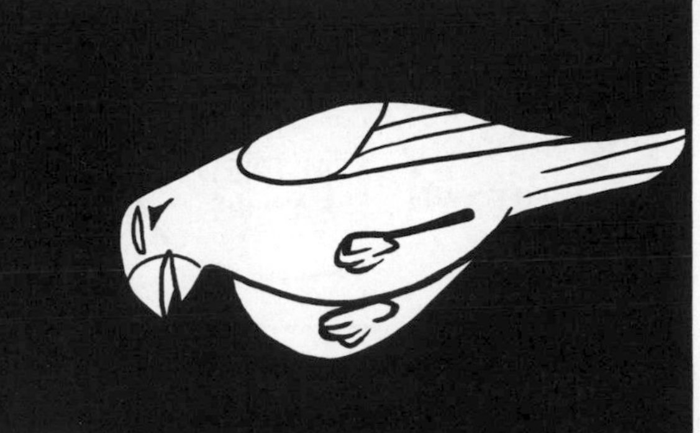

WH-

SORRY FOR THE FRIGHT. YOU OKAY?

AM I OKAY?!
I FAIL AT EVERYTHING, EVEN HITTING A WINDOW...
...AND NOW I'M TALKING TO AN ACTUAL MONSTER.

MONSTER? THAT'S A MEAN THING TO CALL SOMEONE.

I'M IN A MEAN MOOD!
HAVE YOU TRIED... EATING.

I'M A SONGBIRD WHO CAN'T SING.
MY LIFE IS WITHOUT MEANING!
YOU DON'T SAY.
DON'T BELIEVE ME? LISTEN-

THERE YOU GO, ALL MY FLAWS LAID BARE. HURRY UP AND EAT ME, YOU'LL BE DOING ME A FAVOR.

HMM.
NO.
WHAT?!

I HAVE PLENTY OF FOOD.
I ONLY WANT FOR GUESTS.

BUT YOU'RE A MONSTER... YOU'RE SUPPOSED TO KILL ME.

I DON'T CARE WHAT I'M SUPPOSED TO DO.

I'M SUPPOSED TO HUNT, BUT I **DON'T.**
I'M NOT SUPPOSED TO READ, BUT I **DO.**

AND IN THE BEST BOOKS, THE CHARACTERS **NEVER** DO WHAT THEY'RE SUPPOSED TO DO.

ARE BIRDS SUPPOSED TO SING? I'VE ONLY NOTICED THE ONE WHO **CAN'T.**
YOU CAME HERE SEEKING AN END, BUT **MAYBE** YOU STUMBLED ON AN OPPORTUNITY.

BUT I HAVEN'T GOT THE SLIGHTEST IDEA WHERE TO BEGIN.

WELL, IF IT'S IDEAS YOU NEED...

BURROWS

Abby Howard and Eli Church

WHAT DO YOU SEE?

YOU SEEM DREADFULLY FOCUSED.
WHY.
I DON'T KNOW, THAT'S WHY I'M ASKING.

UGH.
WHY ARE YOU NOT DIGGING?

SAME REASON AS YOU.
NOT A DIGGER.

I WAS GIVEN A JOB.
AND I GAVE MYSELF ONE.
ALL THE SAME.

BESIDES, THE ELDER ALREADY WILLS THE REST OF THE WARREN TO SEE IT DONE.

SHUNNING RESPONSIBILITY IS A SIN.
SHUNNING ANYTHING IS A SIN.
UNLESS IT'S FEAR.

FEARED OF DIGGING?
AFEARED OF THE PANIC THE DIGGING PAINTS ON THE WALLS.

IT WILL BE WELL.

SHFF
SHFF
WILL IT...?

WHAT IS THAT?
A FOX.
NO FOX LOOKS AS THAT ONE DOES!
SINCE WHEN ARE YOU THE AUTHORITY ON FOXES?
MAYBE YOU SHOULD LEAVE ME ALONE AND LET ME DECIDE WHAT IS OR ISN'T A FOX AND WHAT IS OR ISN'T WORTH MY ATTENTION!
IT'S GONE.

WHAT?! WHERE DID IT GO?
DID IT RETURN TO THE WOODS...?
NO.
WH-WHAT?
BUT HOW COULD IT—
I'LL GO.
WHAT? BUT YOU CAN'T JUST—
SHUNNING RESPONSIBILITY IS A SIN.

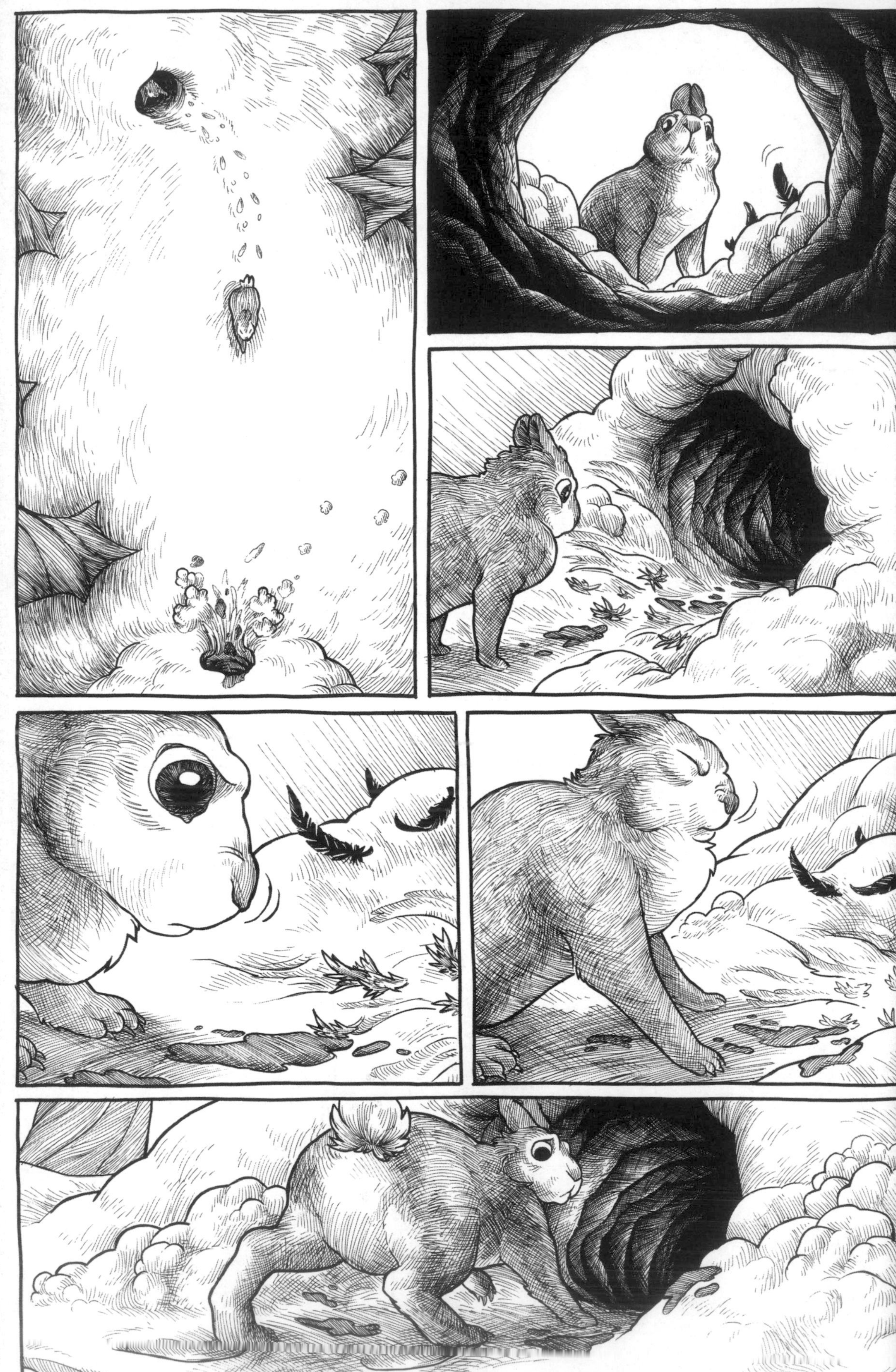

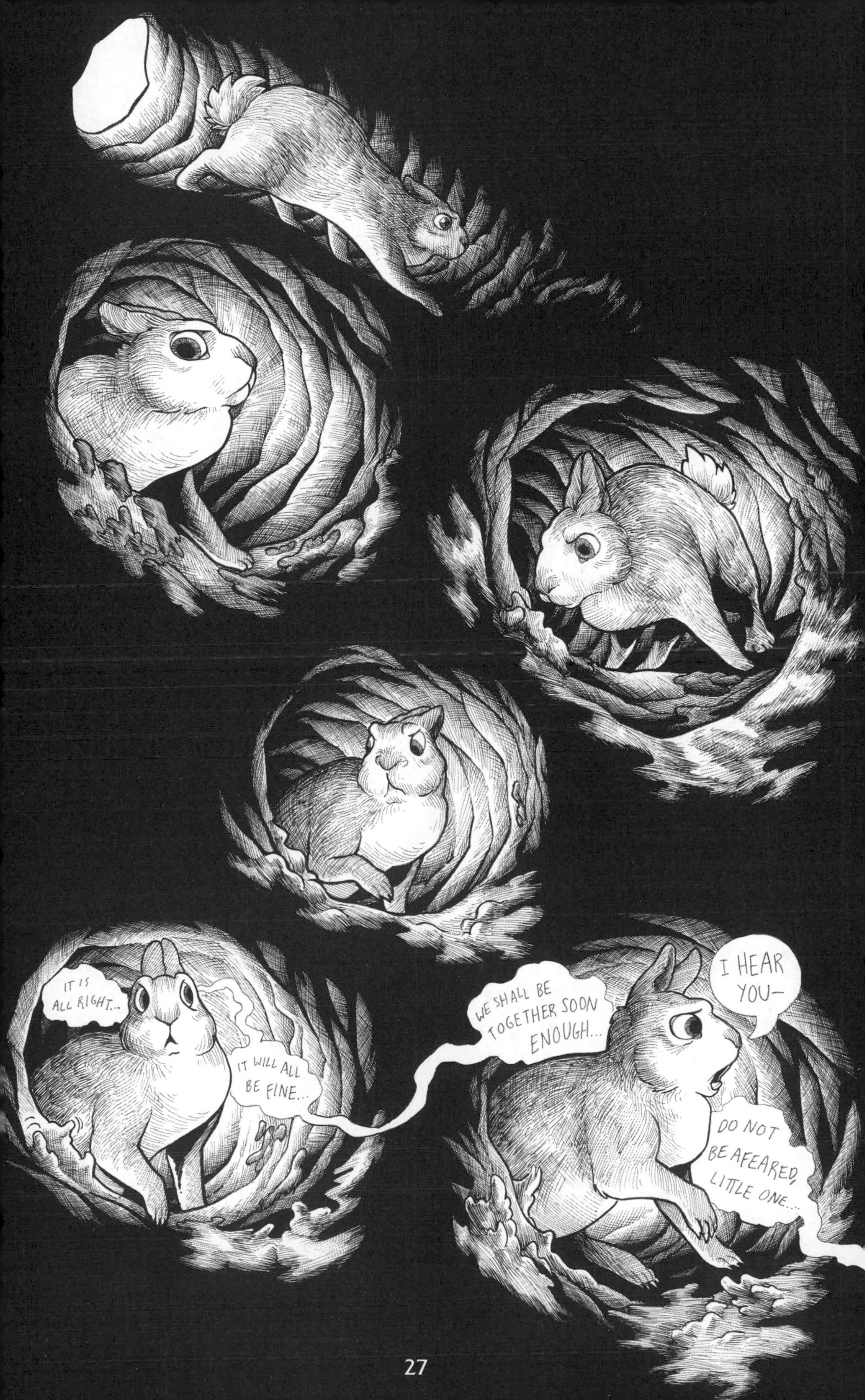
IT IS ALL RIGHT...
IT WILL ALL BE FINE...
WE SHALL BE TOGETHER SOON ENOUGH...
I HEAR YOU–
DO NOT BE AFEARED, LITTLE ONE...

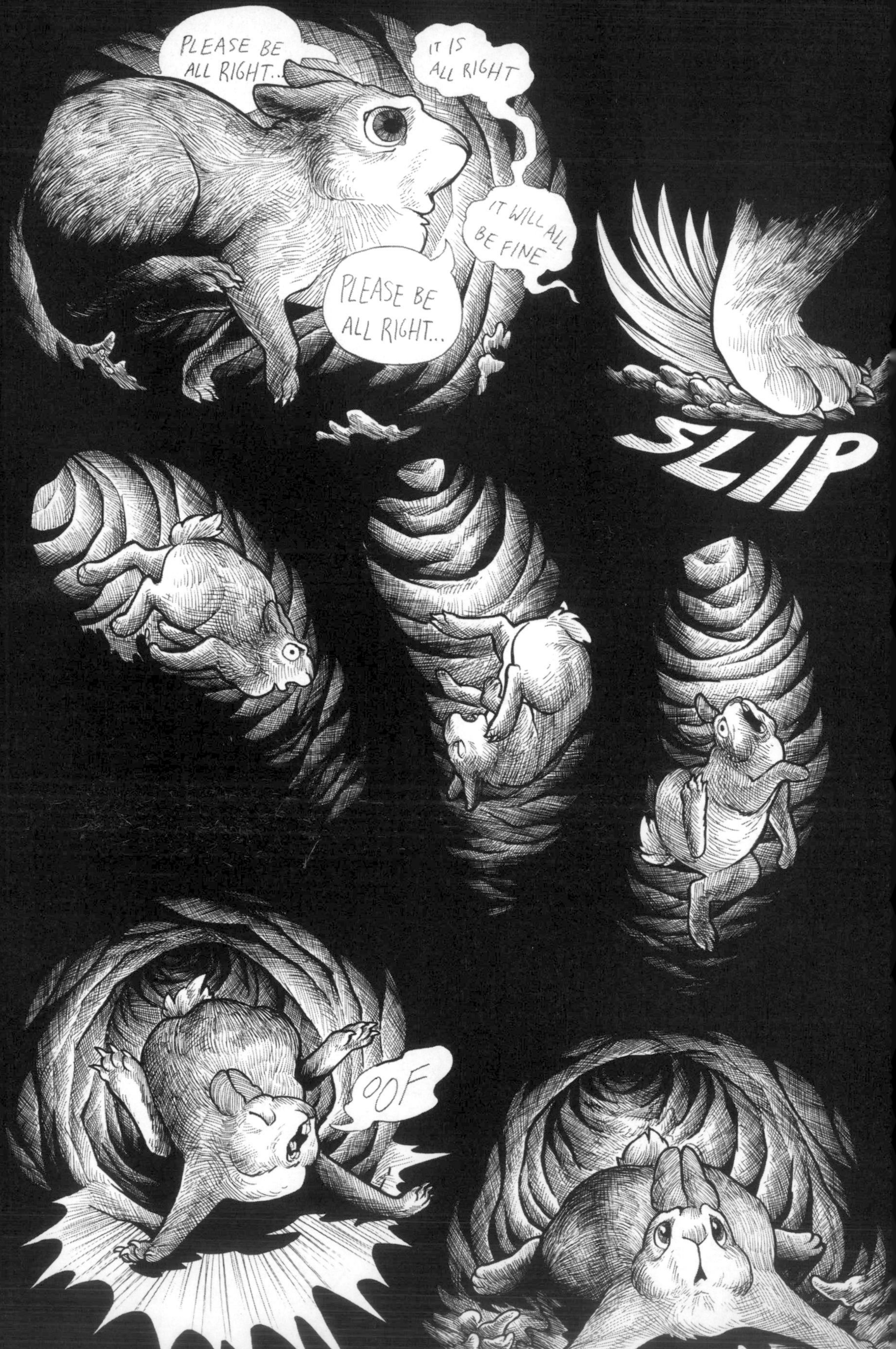

PLEASE BE ALL RIGHT...
IT IS ALL RIGHT
IT WILL ALL BE FINE
PLEASE BE ALL RIGHT...
SLIP
OOF

IT'S ALL RIGHT, ALL WILL BE FINE
DO NOT BE AFEARED, LITTLE ONE....
IT IS ALL RIGHT....
IT WILL ALL BE FINE...
WE SHALL BE TOGETHER SOON ENOUGH.

SKTCH
SKTCH

COME ON, NOW, DIG!

JUST A LITTLE FARTHER NOW!

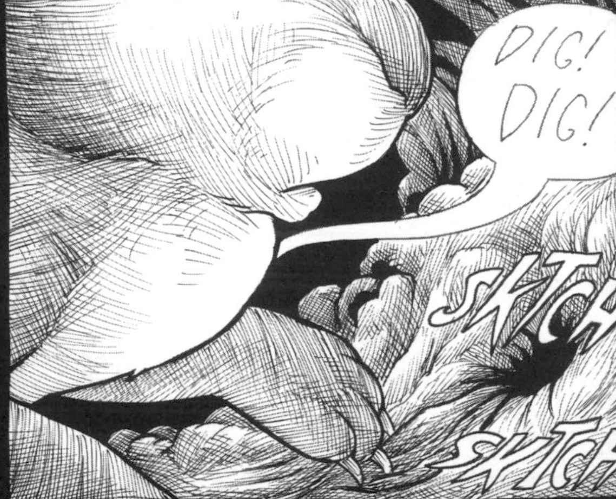
DIG! DIG!
SKTCH
SKTCH

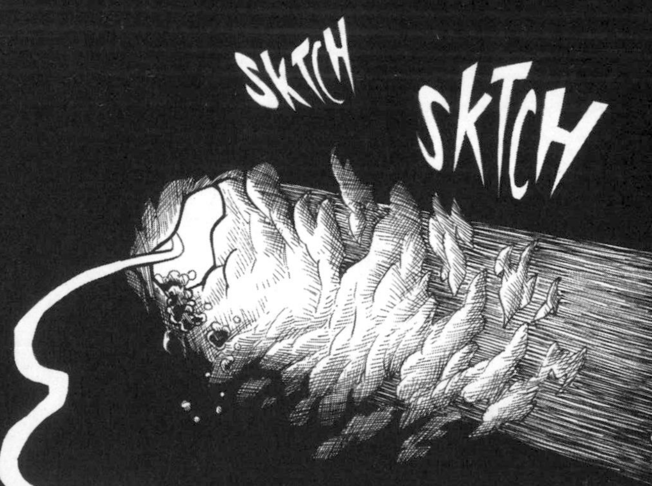
SKTCH
SKTCH
SKTCH
CAN YOU NOT HEAR THEM?
WE WILL BE TOGETHER SOON ENOUGH.

Chosen Ones
BY RYAN ESTRADA
AND RACHEL DUKES

explore

AT LAST, YOU'VE COME. "THE CHOSEN ONE," AS PROPHECIES FORETOLD.
OUR VILLAGE'S FATE HAS LAID IN WAIT AS I HAVE GROWN SO OLD.

FOR MANY A YEAR, WE'VE LIVED IN FEAR, FORCED TO COWER AND HIDE.
A HORRID BEAST, HAS MADE A FEAST, OF ALL WHO GO OUTSIDE.
UNTIL THAT HORRID BEAST IS SLAIN OUR KIND WILL NOT KNOW PEACE AGAIN. BUT NONE COULD BE SO BOLD.
IT WAS WRITTEN IN THE SKIES ONE DAY A HERO WOULD ARISE WHO DOES NOT QUITE FIT THE MOLD.

WITH UNAPPRECIATED STRENGTHS ONE WHO'D GO TO ANY LENGTHS WHEN THEIR BACK'S AGAINST THE WALL.
ONE WHO FEELS DESTINED FOR THEY KNOW NOT WHAT, JUST SOMETHING MORE.
YOU HAVE ANSWERED THAT CALL.
IF YOU CAN LIFT THIS SACRED SWORD, AND CARRY IT ON TOWARD A PLACE BEYOND WHERE YOU'VE EXPLORED.
NOT STOP UNTIL THE BEAST IS GORED. WAR AT END, THE PEACE RESTORED GREATNESS WILL BE YOUR REWARD.

YOU ARE THE ONE. I WISH YOU WELL.
THE ROAD IS LONG, IT WILL BE HELL. BUT
KNOW IN YOUR HEART ONE THING IS TRUE.
NOW THAT WE HAVE FOUND "THE ONE," THIS IMPOSSIBLE FEAT WILL BE DONE.
OUR ONLY HOPE IS YOU!

FATHER, I'VE HEARD YOU TELL THAT LIE TO SO MANY PASSERSBY. NOT ONE'S RETURNED, YOU SEE?
JUST LET ME GO AND I WILL SHOW THE PROPHECY DESCRIBES ME!
DON'T YOU SEE, MY SON, IT DESCRIBES EVERYONE. IT'S WHAT THEY ALREADY BELIEVE:
"YOU'RE UNIQUE, NOT JUST STRANGE! THE WORLD'S YOURS TO CHANGE! YOU'RE SPECIAL, NOT SIMPLY NAIVE."

BUT IF I TELL ENOUGH PEOPLE THAT TRIPE, MAYBE ONE OF THEM WILL BE RIGHT. THAT IS VANITY WE CANNOT AFFORD.
NOW, GO ON AND RUN
TO THE PILE OF DEAD CHOSEN ONES.
I'M OUT OF SACRED SWORDS.

CHIMERA

Aliza Layne and Natalie Riess

no!

there is so much to be done!

where is our head architect?

lance-architect hazel, your grace.

hazel!

yes, how could I forget!

I have so many plans!

yes, I'd started drafting the ones we had discussed before you left, and-

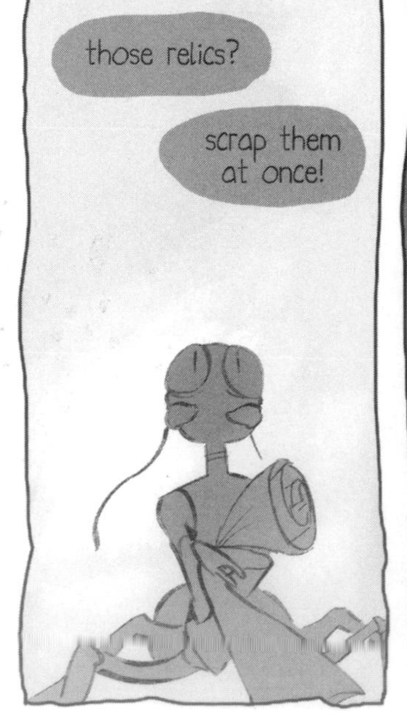

CONSTRUCTION BEGINS.

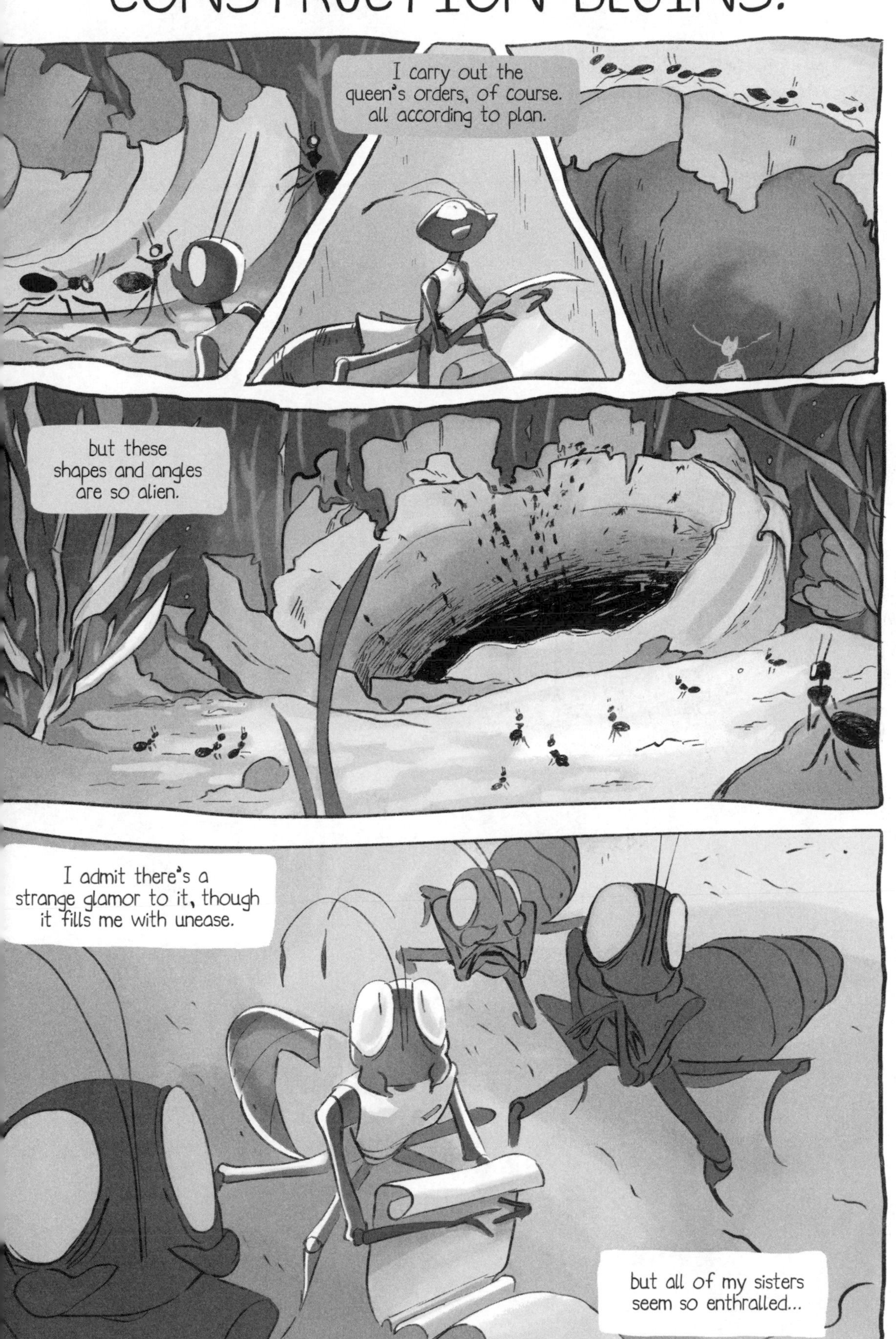

They don't seem to mind the queen's harsher demands and increasing reclusiveness.
...hazel...
...approach...
your highness, I...
...come close

...you want to know...
...what we're building.
my queen?
hhh
hh
hhhhh...c...
..closer...
closer
hh
imagine...
arcs and curved
aper tiers, tumultous and
graceful as the ocean...
rather than below as the ants always have dug...
a cathedral's dome to the heavens...!
my queen, I don't understand–
your queen understands.

hazel
hazel
WHY CAN'T YOU, HAZEL?
hazel
ah
hazel
our queen!
she's-
can't you see it's not her?!
SLAM!

NO!
hm
I BUILT THESE CELLS
I CANNOT BE TRAPPED BY THEM!
WE BUILT THEM NEAR THE ARMORY...

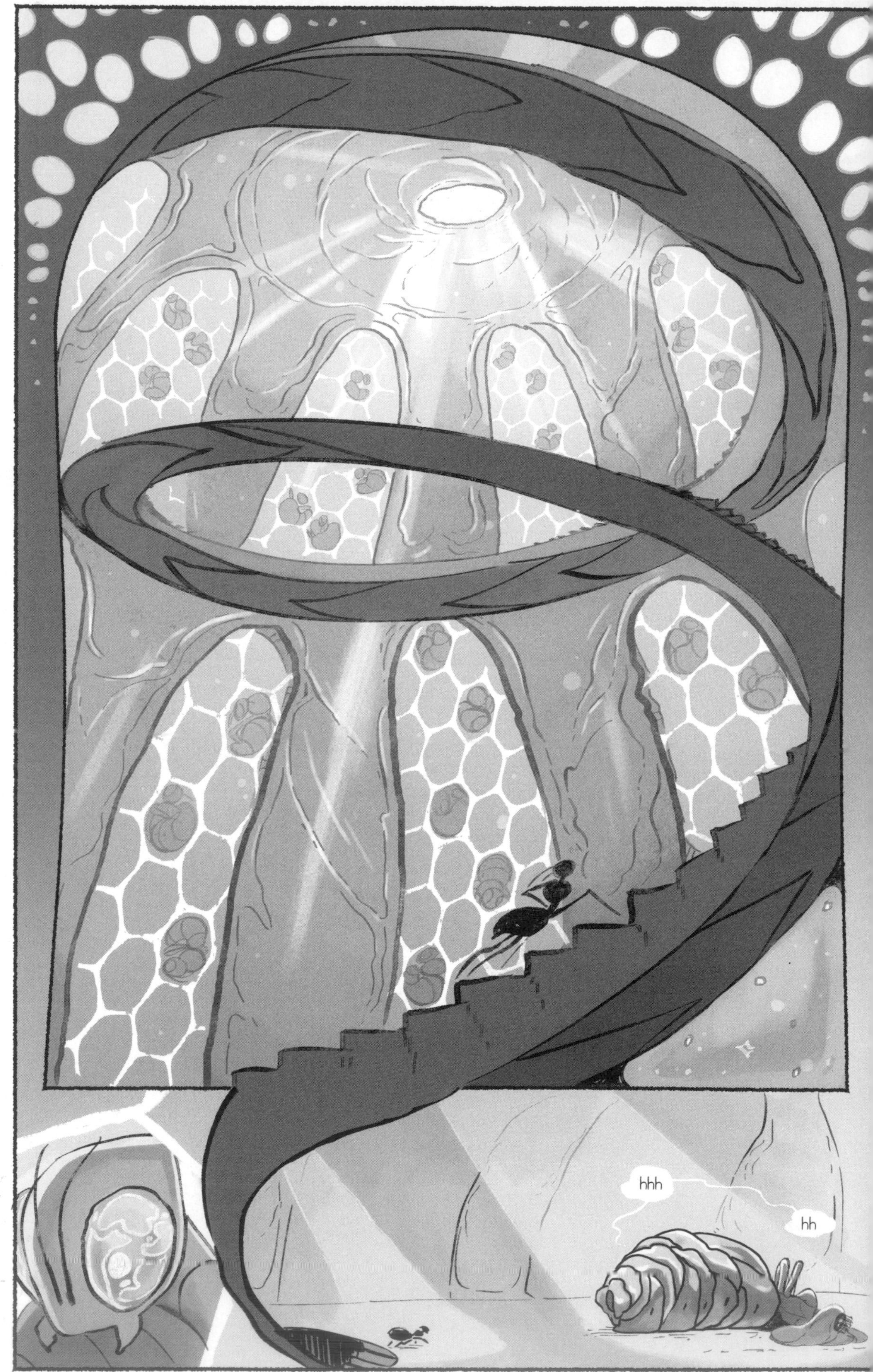
hhh
hh

SPRIT
YOU MUST THINK I'M A MONSTER
DONT YOU?

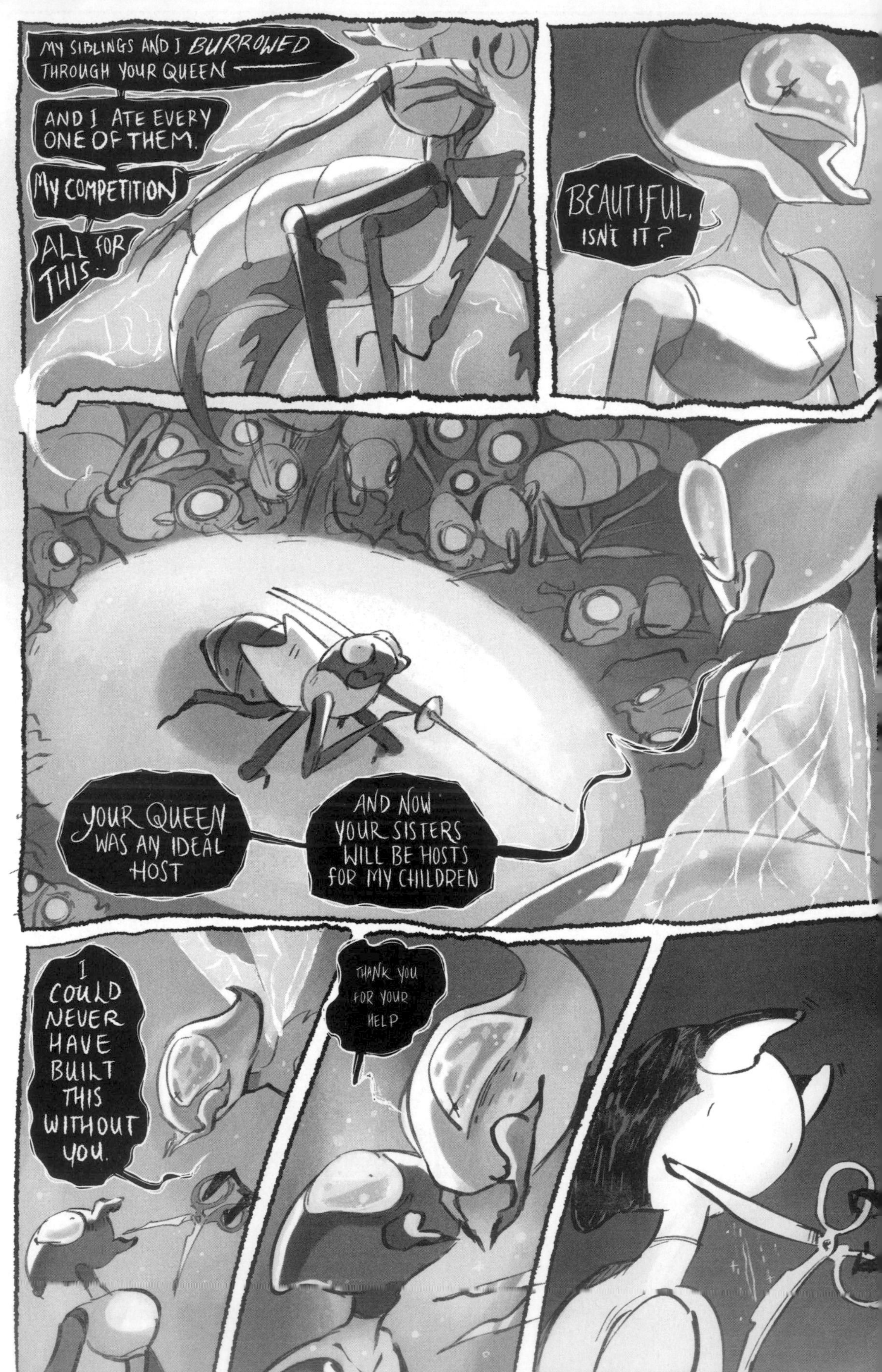
MY SIBLINGS AND I BURROWED THROUGH YOUR QUEEN
AND I ATE EVERY ONE OF THEM.
MY COMPETITION
ALL FOR THIS..
BEAUTIFUL, ISN'T IT?
YOUR QUEEN WAS AN IDEAL HOST
AND NOW YOUR SISTERS WILL BE HOSTS FOR MY CHILDREN
I COULD NEVER HAVE BUILT THIS WITHOUT YOU.
THANK YOU FOR YOUR HELP

CLANG!!
SKRRT

SNAP
OH, MY HAZEL...

someone has
to recoup.
SOMEONE HAS TO
REBUILD...
the end

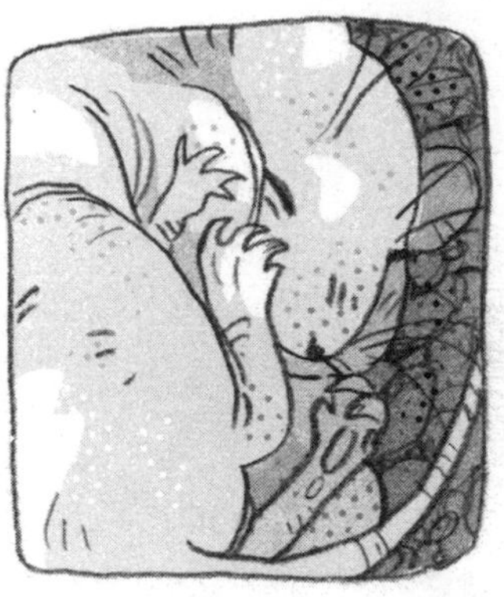

The Flavour of the Sky

Ana Sabater

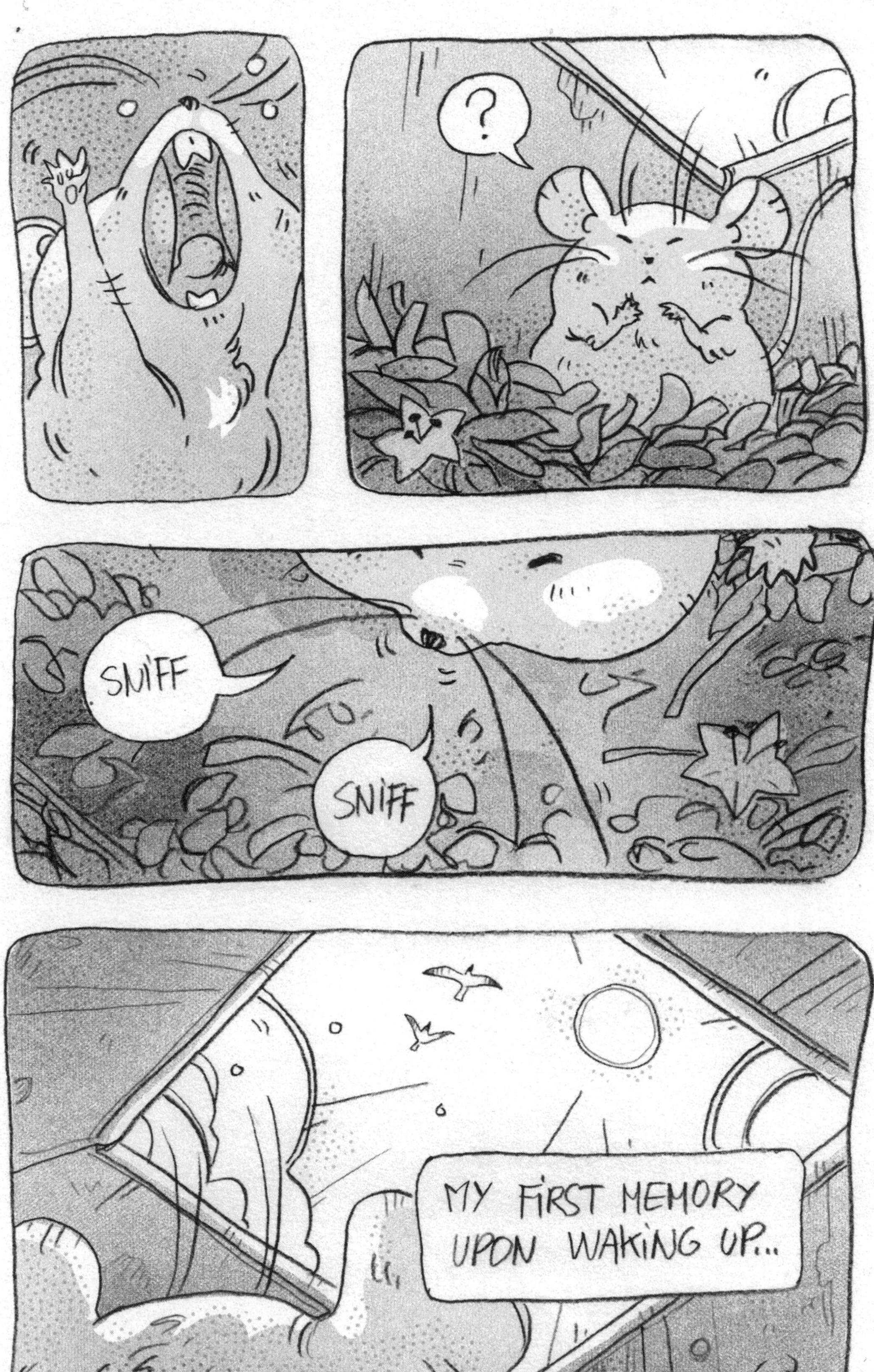
?
SNIFF
SNIFF
MY FIRST MEMORY UPON WAKING UP...

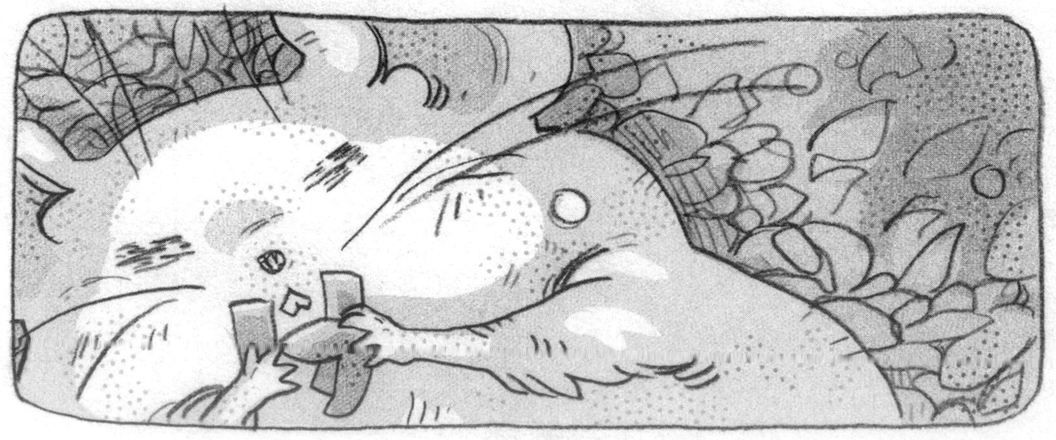

TIME TEA

EEK
!

EEEK!
Ceylon Tea

-Ri!
TORI!
DID YOU FIND SOMEONE?
AYE!
A CASTAWAY MOUSE.
BUT HE SEEMS JUST FINE.
HE'S NOT WAKING UP?
BLAST!
TORI, MICE ARE NOT MEANT TO FLY!
WELL, I COULDN'T LEAVE HIM THERE!
AND WE SHOULDN'T STAY HERE.
I WILL TAKE CARE OF HIM.

INDEED.
THERE ARE TOO MANY PEOPLE.
I WILL BRING HIM TO MY PLACE.
BE CAREFUL, TORI.

TICK
TOCK
Camus
LA PESTE
CAMUS - LA PESTE
TICK
TOCK
MY FIRST MEMORY UPON WAKING UP...
TICK
...WAS BEING IN A CAN MADE OF TIN...
TOCK

WELL, YOU FINALLY WOKE UP.
MY NAME IS PROSERPINA.
HOW ARE YOU FEE--
EEK!
NO!!
EEK!
I DON'T MEAN TO HARM YOU!
STOP! CALM DOWN, YOU'RE SAFE HERE!
EEK!!
EEK!
EEEK!!

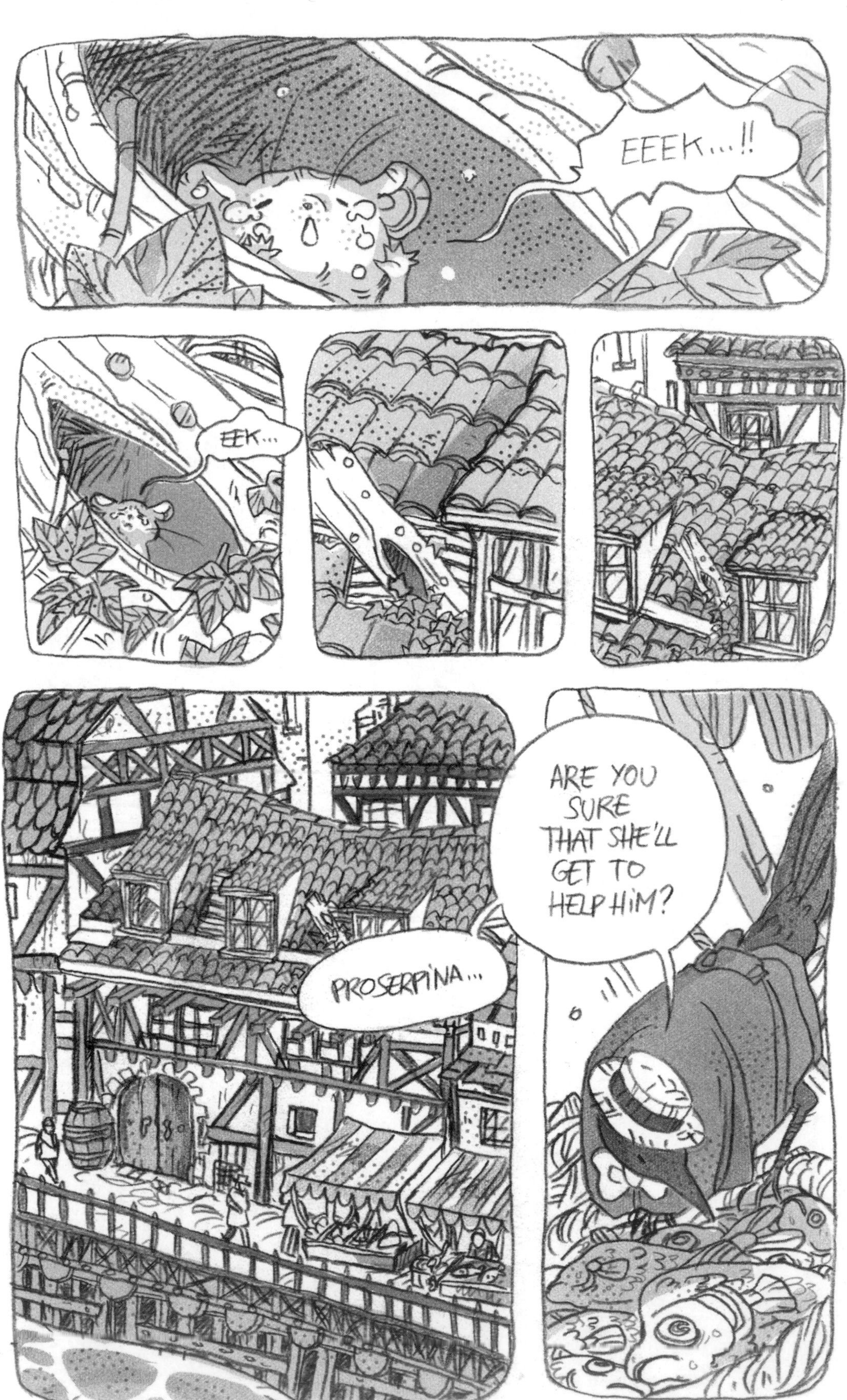
EEEK...!!
EEK...
PROSERPINA...
ARE YOU SURE THAT SHE'LL GET TO HELP HIM?

I DON'T HAVE A BETTER PLAN.
AND I CAN'T JUST LEAVE THE MOUSE LIKE THAT.
HE WOULDN'T LAST A DAY.
BUT WHAT ARE WE GOING TO DO...
DON'T YOU EVEN MENTION THAT.
IF TORI DOESN'T SHOW UP?
BLAST.
BIRD OF ILL OMEN.
IS IT THAT BAD?
HE JUST KEEPS ON BITING AND SNIFFING EVERYTHING.
AND HE LOOKS AT THE SKY...
I THINK HE'S LOOKING FOR SOMETHING HE HAD WHEN TORI FOUND HIM.
EEK...

UNBELIEVABLE.
I LEAVE YOU ALONE FOR A MOMENT...
EEK!
YOU CAN'T STRIP OFF YOUR CLOTHES CONSTANTLY.
EEK!
EEK!
OH, YOU EVEN SNAPPED A BUTTON.
EEK!
STAY PUT.
EEK!
WE'LL ADD A RIBBON FOR MAXIMUM SECURITY.
PERFECT!

YOU MUST LEARN TO BEHAVE.
...
SIGH.
LISTEN, I HAVEN'T FOUND TORI YET.
EEK!
TASTES LIKE SKY
I CAN'T JUST GUESS WHAT WAS IN YOUR BOX.
AND I CAN'T GO OUT EVERY DAY BECAUSE OF IT.
EEK...
TOMORROW GALA WILL HELP YOU INSTEAD.
?
YES, GALA.

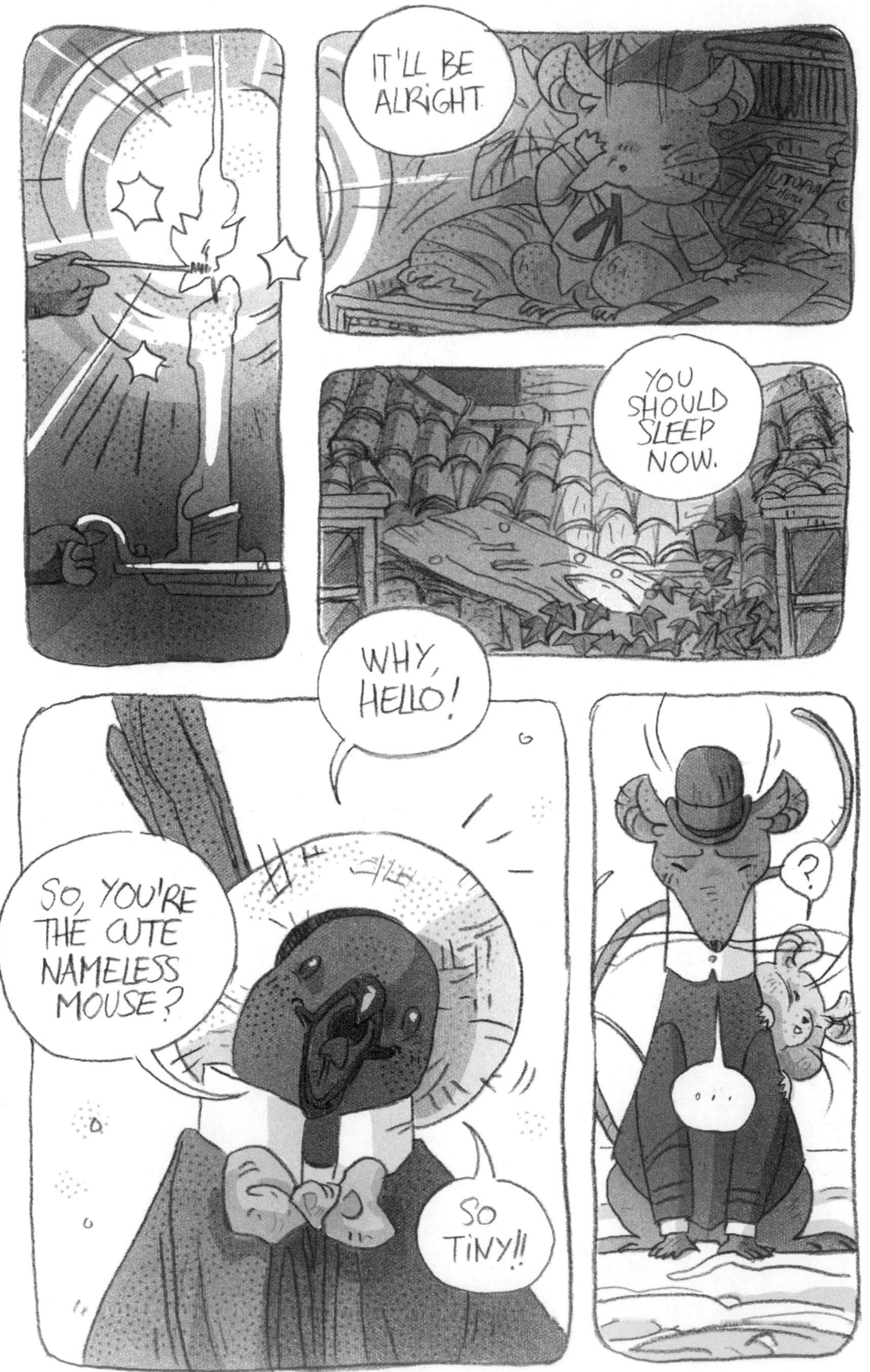
IT'LL BE ALRIGHT.
YOU SHOULD SLEEP NOW.
WHY, HELLO!
SO, YOU'RE THE CUTE NAMELESS MOUSE?
SO TINY!!
?
...

WELL, YOU SEE... TORI COULD BE ANYWHERE...
EEK!
YOU MISS THE FLAVOUR?
AS FAR AS I KNOW, THE SKY DOESN'T TASTE LIKE ANYTHING.
BUT...
I WILL HELP YOU FIND WHAT YOU HAVE LOST.

YOU DON'T LIKE...
...THE FLAVOUR ...
HO
...OF ANYTHING?

eeuuinkel ~ Tea Sho
AH!

WAIT!!

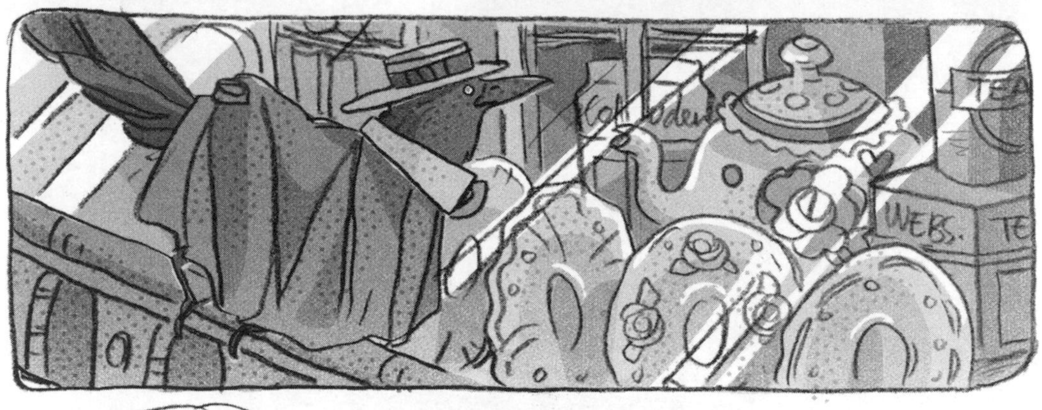

WEBS.

OH, NO...
LITTLE MOUSE ...

TEA
TEA
TEA
Mint Tea
CEYLON
SABA
SNIFF
CEYLON FINEST TEA LEAVES
EEK!
LOOSE LEAVES

TEA
EEEK...?
SNIFF
!?
SNIFF
BLACK TEA
SNIFF!
EEK!
SNIFF

HA!
YOU HAD ME DEAD WORRIED!
EH?
Tea
OH, NO... DON'T CRY...
LET'S FIND PROSERPINA, ALRIGHT?
EEK...
SO... AFTER ALL ...
IT WAS TEA WHAT HE LOOKED FOR...
EEK...
YES.
I THINK...
HE FOUND WHAT HE WANTED...
BUT NOT THE WAY HE WANTED IT...

SO...
IN THE END YOU DIDN'T FIND THE RIGHT TEA?
BUT THERE'S NO REASON TO BE SAD.
YOU COULD CREATE YOUR OWN TEA.
MAKE YOUR OWN FLAVOUR OF THE SKY.
IN THIS WAY, YOU COULD EVEN LET OTHERS DISCOVER...
...WHAT YOU FOUND AT THE SEA.
EEK!
SO CRY NO MORE...
EEK.

MY FIRST MEMORY UPON WAKING UP WAS BEING IN A CAN MADE OF TIN FULL OF TEA...
SO I DECIDED TO CALL MYSELF TIM O'TEA.
... YOU'RE FREE NOW.
TEA TALES
FINEST TEA
AND ONE DAY I WILL FIND MY SKY.
OR RA

-FIN-

LONG AGO, CREATURES OF ALL KINDS CAME TO THIS RIVER SEEKING SANCTUARY FROM A GREAT STORM OF FIRE.
WHAT THEY FOUND WAS AN ARMY HIDING IN THE BLACK MURK...
AN ARMY LED BY AN ANCIENT KING.
THERE'S BEEN AN ACCIDENT.
IT'S ROHO.
THE CARNAGE LASTED UNTIL THE CREATURES OF THE LAND BANDED TOGETHER AND STRUCK A BARGAIN WITH THE KING OF THE RIVER.
BROTHER?
THE FAR SHORE
BY WILL STRODE + LINDSEY LEA
SO LONG AS WE REMAINED ON HIS SHORES, THE SOULS OF OUR DEAD WOULD RETURN TO THE CROSSINGS AND OFFER THEMSELVES FOR JUDGMENT.
HE'S KILLED HIM.
WHAT HAVE YOU DONE, ROHO?!
THE BOY AGAIN.
ROTTEN TO THE CORE.
THE UNWORTHY WOULD NOT.
THE MEEK AND THE PURE WOULD BE ALLOWED SAFE PASSAGE TO THE LANDS OF THE DEAD.
THE BOY HAS DOOMED US!

PEACE BETWEEN THE TRIBES WAS BUILT ON FEAR AND COMPLIANCE.

THE PRICE FOR ENDANGERING THAT PEACE HAD BEEN IMPRESSED UPON US SINCE BIRTH...

A CURSE PASSED DOWN FROM THE OLD WORLD TO ENSURE A COMMITMENT TO THE KING'S WISHES.

A CURSE OF EXILE AND GNAWING DEATH.

I CANNOT IMAGINE THE CRUELTY REQUIRED TO CREATE SUCH A SPELL...

NOR THE EVEN GREATER CRUELTY REQUIRED TO USE IT

HE PRIESTESS OLD US THAT HE CURSE VOULD TAKE OLD BEFORE HE SUN FELL N THE SECOND AY...
THERE ARE A HOUSAND THINGS OUT HERE THAT COULD KILL YOU, MOYO.
THE KING HIMSELF COULD SWALLOW US WHOLE IN AN INSTANT.
I'M NOT GOING BACK.
STUBBORN OX...
ARDS.
IDIOTS.
ROHO, COME TAKE A BREAK. I'VE FOUND SOME MANGOES...
SAVE YOUR PITY, SISTER.
WE MUST KEEP MOVING.
BUT I SAW THE CHANGE IN HIM RIGHT AWAY.
HIS ANGER WAS MORE THAN OUTRAGE.
IT CONSUMED HIM.
T TRUDGED LONGSIDE S LEAVING EEPER RINTS VITH VERY TEP.
MURDERER!
CURSED!
OUTCAST!
STOP IT! LEAVE HIM ALONE!
WHO ASKED YOU TO DEFEND ME?
WE SHOULD WAIT UNTIL MORNING.
NONE OF YOU WANT ME.
DID YOU HEAR ME? THIS ISN'T SAFE.
NONE OF YOU.
BY THE TIME WE REACHED THE KING'S BRIDGE, MY BROTHER SEEMED TO LEAVE NO TRACKS AT ALL.
THE BRIDGE...
YOU KNOW WHAT WILL HAPPEN.
WE CAN'T GO ANY FURTHER.
LL THAT WAS EFT WAS A REATURE VITHOUT ARE OR EAR...
A CONDITION I GREW TO ENVY.
YOU'RE RIGHT.
YOU CAN'T.

I CAN HEAR THE LAND OF THE DEAD CALLING AND YOU ARE NOT WELCOME.
YOU AREN'T MAKING ANY SENSE!
WE CAN MAKE A **RAFT**.
WE CAN...
WE CAN--

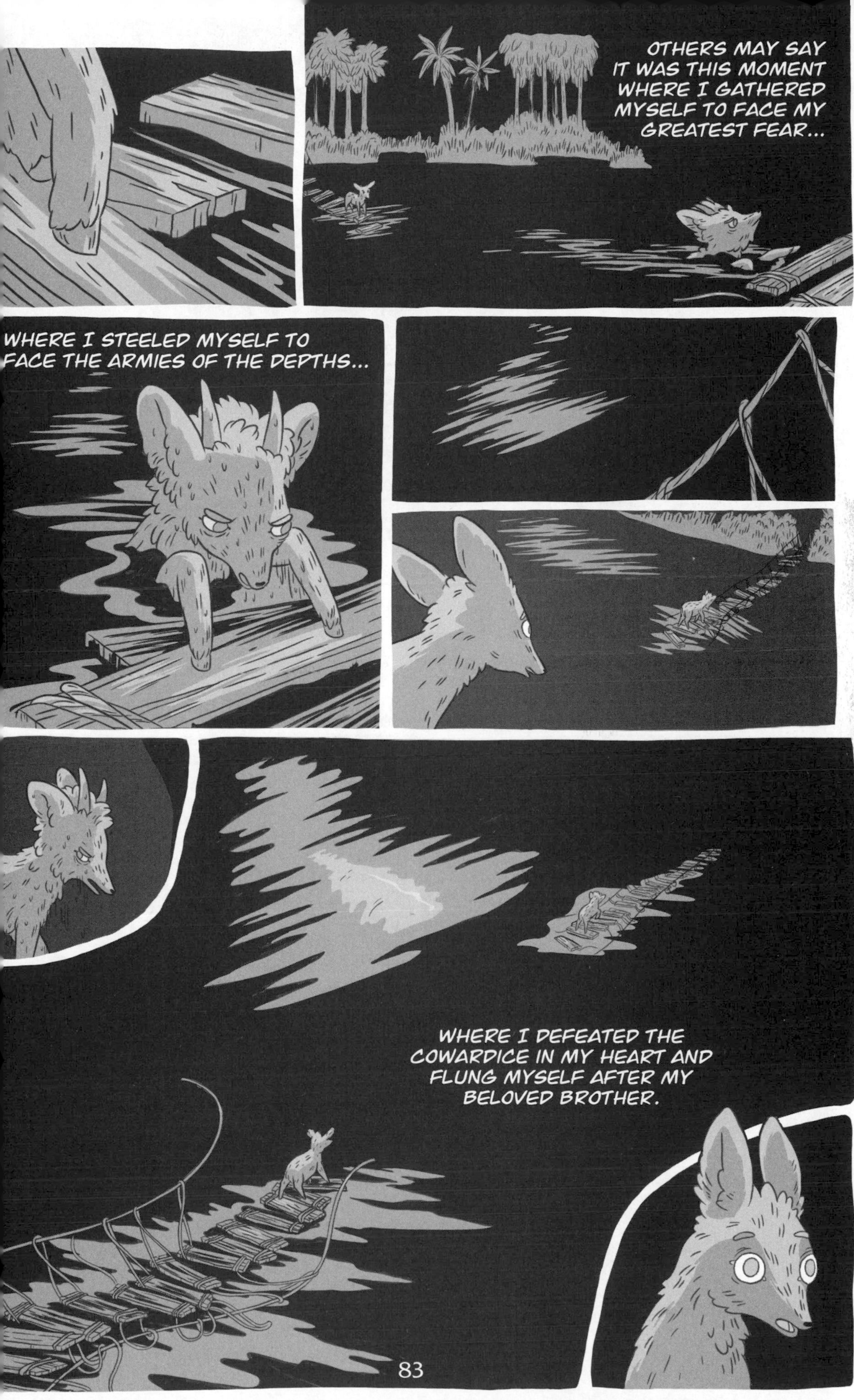
OTHERS MAY SAY IT WAS THIS MOMENT WHERE I GATHERED MYSELF TO FACE MY GREATEST FEAR...
WHERE I STEELED MYSELF TO FACE THE ARMIES OF THE DEPTHS...
WHERE I DEFEATED THE COWARDICE IN MY HEART AND FLUNG MYSELF AFTER MY BELOVED BROTHER.

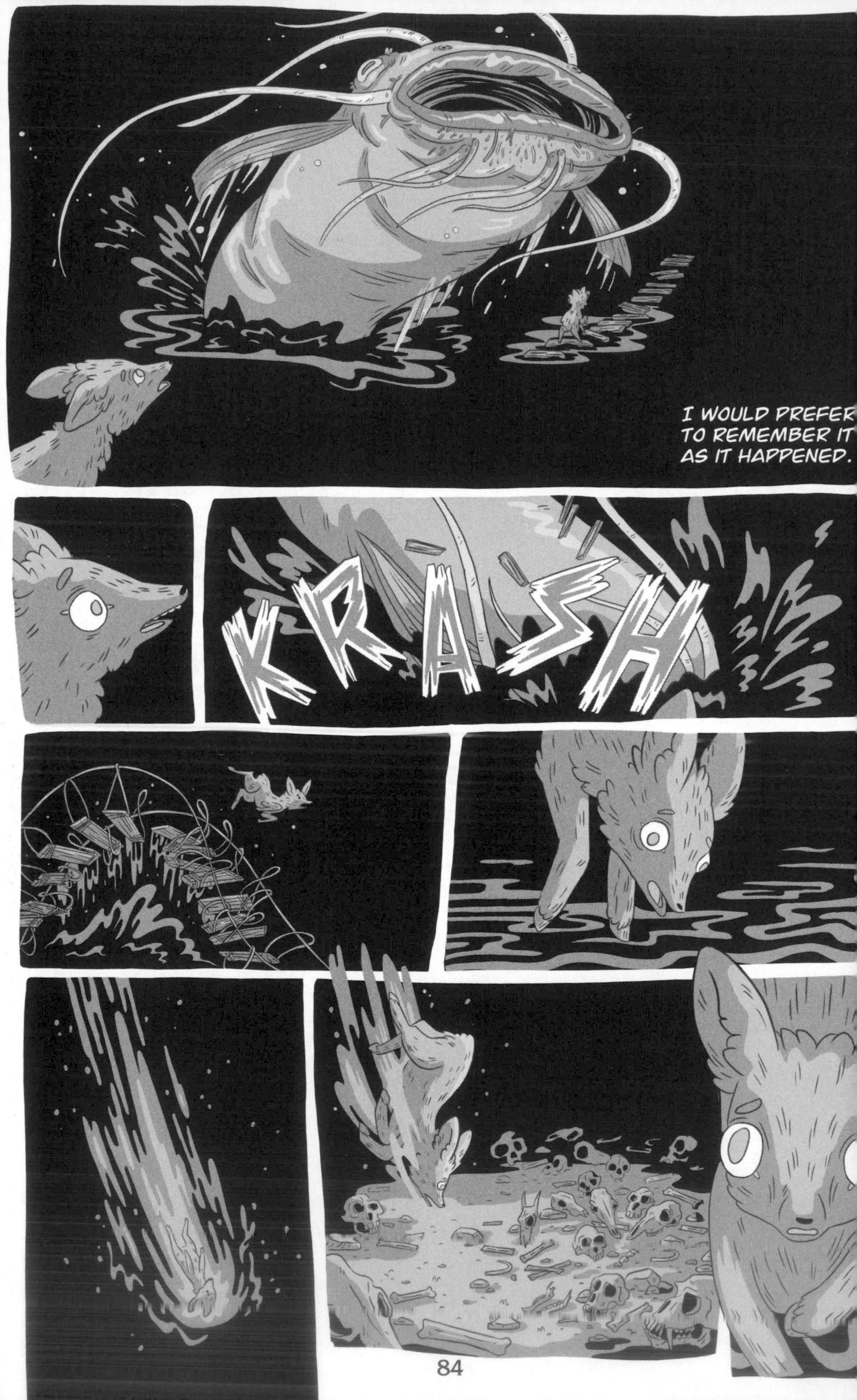
I WOULD PREFER TO REMEMBER IT AS IT HAPPENED.
KRASH

THERE WAS NO GREAT SWELL OF STRENGTH IN MY BOSOM.
ONLY A DEEP AND ANCIENT FEAR...
AND SOMEWHERE BEYOND IT...
NO...
NO!
FURY.

UGH...
ROHO!
KAHK
KAH
KAHK
KAK
KAAK
KAH
KASHL
KAHK
KAHK

KAHK
KASHL
KAK
KAHK
KAK
KAHK
KASHL
KAK
HROOOOOOSH

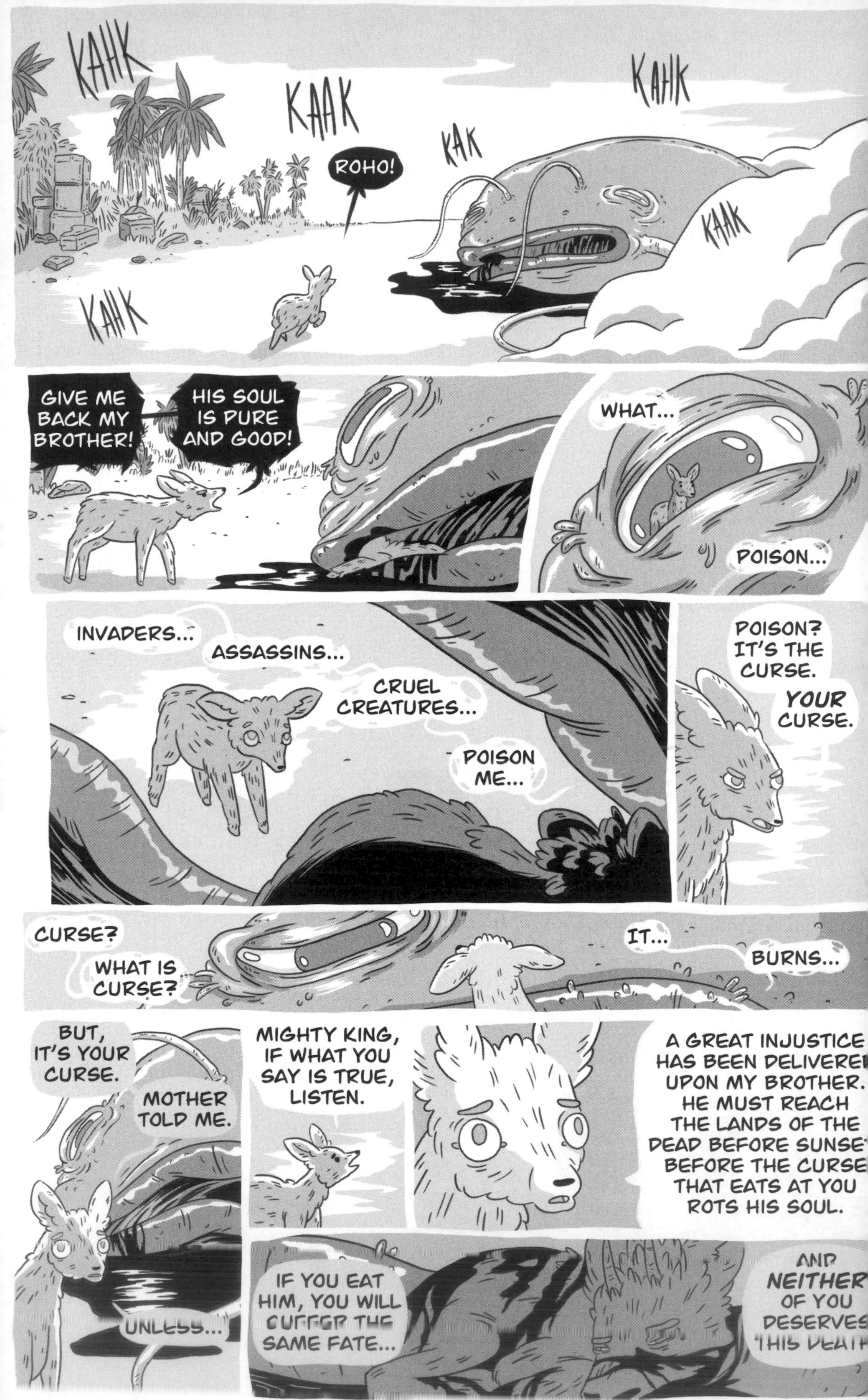
KAHK
KAAK
KAHK
KAK
ROHO!
KAAK
KAHK
GIVE ME BACK MY BROTHER!
HIS SOUL IS PURE AND GOOD!
WHAT...
POISON...
INVADERS...
ASSASSINS...
CRUEL CREATURES...
POISON ME...
POISON? IT'S THE CURSE.
YOUR CURSE.
CURSE?
WHAT IS CURSE?
IT...
BURNS...
BUT, IT'S YOUR CURSE.
MOTHER TOLD ME.
MIGHTY KING, IF WHAT YOU SAY IS TRUE, LISTEN.
A GREAT INJUSTICE HAS BEEN DELIVERED UPON MY BROTHER. HE MUST REACH THE LANDS OF THE DEAD BEFORE SUNSET BEFORE THE CURSE THAT EATS AT YOU ROTS HIS SOUL.
UNLESS...
IF YOU EAT HIM, YOU WILL SUFFER THE SAME FATE...
AND NEITHER OF YOU DESERVES THIS DEATH

GROOOWR
SAVE ME..
MY CHILDREN...
NEED ME...
I WILL.
I CAN SAVE YOU.
I CAN.
HE WAS TRYING TO SAVE ME.
THE BOY.
I WANTED TO SHOW HIM I COULD CLIMB THE TREES AS HE DID.
WE WENT SO HIGH, SISTER.
BUT I SLIPPED.
HE FELL WITH ME.
I KILLED HIM.
HE WAS MY ONLY FRIEND AND I KILLED HIM.
NO, THIS IS THE KING...
NO, BROTHER. HE WASN'T.
CAN YOU HEAR ME?
..YOU...

YOU SAVED ME...
TELL...
WANT.
PLEASE VISIT OUR PEOPLE. TELL THEM THE CURSES MUST STOP.
I WILL DO...
AS YOU ASK...
WE CAN'T LEAVE HIM THIS WAY.
COME, BROTHER.
WE STILL HAVE TIME.

THE SUN IS FALLING.
WE'RE ALMOST THERE.
CAN YOU GO A LITTLE FASTER?
I'LL TRY.
THE KING WASN'T SO SCARY.
MAYBE THIS NEW LAND WON'T BE SO BAD EITHER.
MAYBE WE'LL FIND FIELDS OF WARM TALL GRASS WHERE WE CAN RUN AND PLAY AND EAT UNTIL OUR BELLIES ARE FULL.
WHAT DO YOU THINK?
ROHO?

I OFTEN WONDER WHAT THEY SAY ABOUT US.
I IMAGINE THEY TELL TALES WARNING OF ROHO'S TRAGIC DESTINY.
OF MY OWN FALL TO MISGUIDED LOYALTY.
IT MAKES ME SAD TO THINK OF THEM ALL...
TRAPPED
THEIR TINY GROV
BY FEAR AN
OLD STORIE
WHEN THEY NEEDED ONLY CROSS THE RIVER TO FIND AN ENTIRELY NEW WORLD.

a long way
SARAH O'DONNELL

A DREADFUL DREAM...
WHAT COULD IT MEAN?
OH NO!
IT'S ALMOST TIME FOR US TO OPEN!
HIDE-SAN! GET THE WATER ON FOR TEA!
ROGER!
MORNING, YOSHI-SAN! I JUST TOOK THE BREAD OUT OF THE OVEN.
GREAT! CAN YOU GET THE TRIBUTE READY?
YOU GOT IT!

TAKK
TAKK

BOM
GOOD DAY! HERE FOR TRIBUTES!
COMING!

HERE YOU GO. WE SCRAPED TOGETHER WHAT WE COULD, BUT...

...THE TRIBUTES SEEM MORE FREQUENT THESE DAYS.

THANKS MUCH! SEE YOU TOMORROW!
THERE'S AN EXTRA SANDWICH IN THERE FOR YOU TOO.

A LIFESAVER INDEED!

AT LEAST WE HAVE THIS PLACE THANKS TO YOSHI-SAN.

RUNNING A WESTERN-STYLE CAFE IN LORD BULL'S TERRITORY. HOW DARING!

I-I STILL RESPECT THE OLD WAYS!

RING

WELCOME!

GOOD AFTERNOON.

MIGHT WE BE ALLOWED SOME PRIVACY?

I NEED YOUR HELP.
ME!?

I HAVE A PACKAGE THAT NEEDS TO GET DELIVERED.

IT MUST BE YOU.
BUT MY CAFE... AND THE TRIBUTES...!

IF WE PULL THIS OFF, TRIBUTES WILL BE A THING OF THE PAST. NO MORE SQUABBLING OVER FOOD.
CLAP CLAP
THAT.. WOULD HELP SO MANY OF US... BUT HOW ?

THIS IS WHERE I'LL MEET YOU. PREPARE WELL. YOU WON'T BE OF ANY USE HALF-STARVED OR INJURED.
DON'T ASSUME THAT I'M JUST GOING TO GO!
AND YET
DON'T WORRY, YOSHI-SAN!
I'LL KEEP THINGS UNDER CONTROL!
BUT... BUT...
I'VE NEVER BEEN THIS FAR FROM HOME BEFORE.
MY GRAND-PARENTS CAME A LONG WAY FROM THE COUNTRY.
ALL TO GET CLOSER TO THE CITY WHERE WE DON'T HAVE TO LIVE HAND TO MOUTH.

AM I
UNDOING
THEIR WORK?
WHAT...
WHAT IF...

SLINK
BAM!

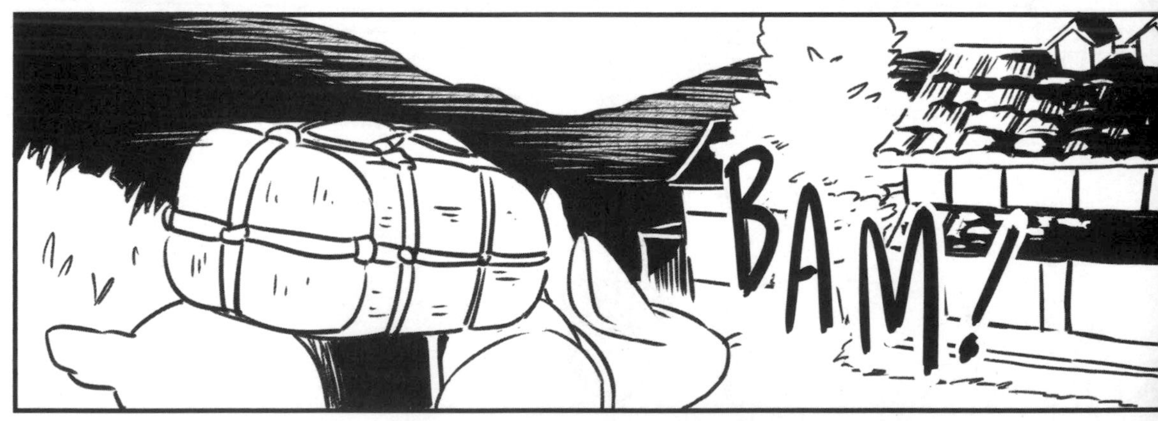
BAM!

SLAM!!

HO...

SUMO?
BAM!

HUP!

GASP

P-PLEASE! ONE MORE MATCH!
THAT WAS BEST OUTTA THREE.

EITHER PAY UP OR BECOME MY AFTERNOON SNACK!
I-IT'S LORD BULL! HIS TRIBUTES HAVE BECOME TOO EXPENSIVE, I CAN'T...

JUST ONE MORE MATCH! IF I CAN BEAT YOU THEN--
WHAM!
TOO LITTLE, TOO LATE.

W-WAIT! PLEASE!
HM ?

HUH. A FRIEND OF FROG'S?
WILL YOU SPARE HIM AND TAKE THIS INSTEAD?

FINE BY ME. SURPRISED THIS HASN'T GONE STRAIGHT TO LORD BULL.
I'VE ALREADY PAID MY TRIBUTE.

HEH, WELL, DON'T LET HIM GET WORD THAT YOU'VE EXTRA TO SPARE.

I'M NOT GOING TO PAY YOU BACK! I'VE STILL GOT FIGHT IN ME LEFT!
EASY, NOW. I JUST WANTED TO HELP--

PLEASE! I'VE NOTHING LEFT. MIGHT I OFFER MY PROTECTION IN EXCHANGE FOR FOOD?
THAT WAS MY LAST SANDWICH BEFORE I STARTED FORAGING...

WE'RE ALL GOING TO DIE ON THIS JOURNEY TOGETHER
I-I MEAN I CAN ALWAYS MAKE MORE! IF YOU HAVE ACCESS TO A KITCHEN...

A KITCHEN?
HEH...

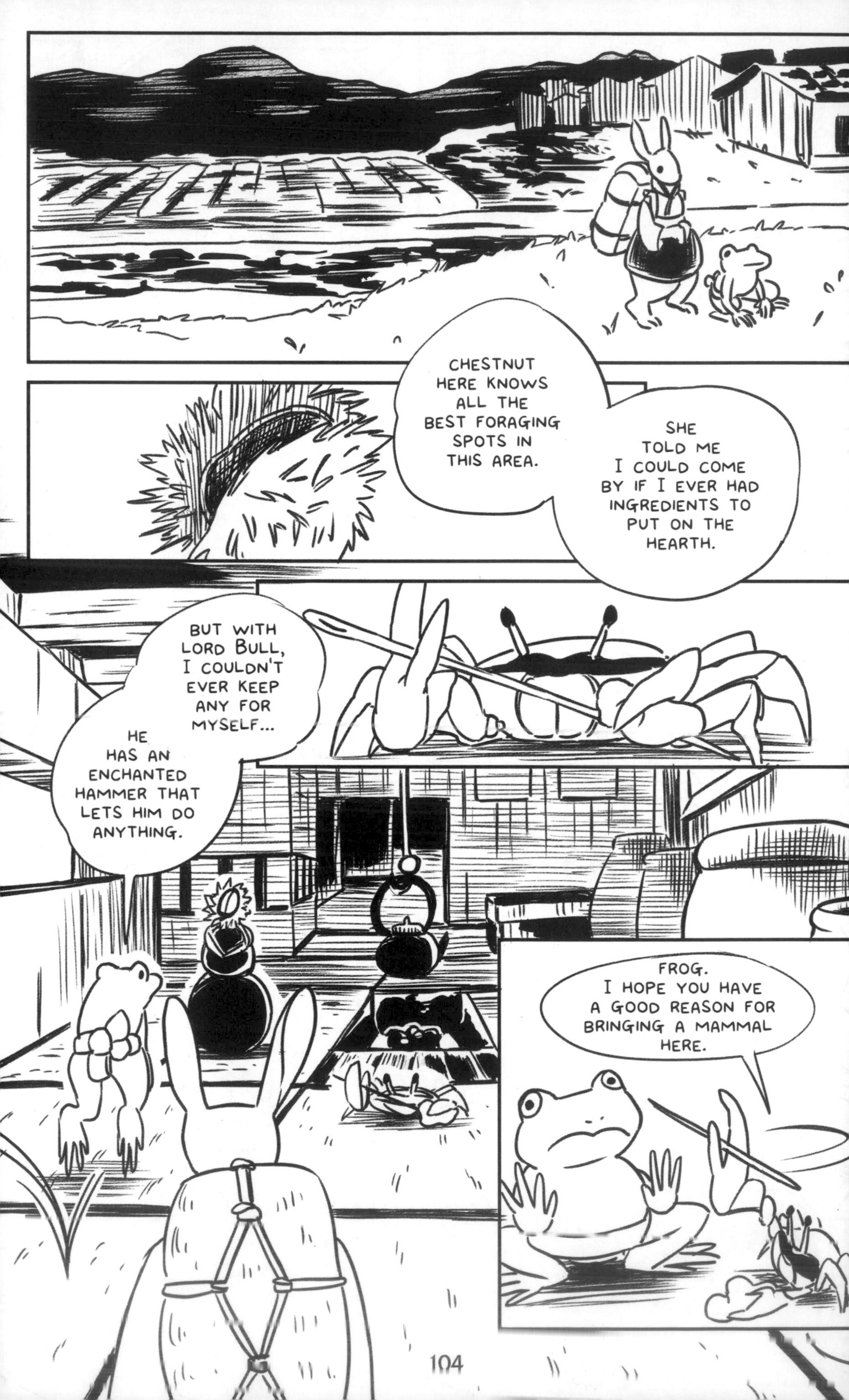
CHESTNUT HERE KNOWS ALL THE BEST FORAGING SPOTS IN THIS AREA.
SHE TOLD ME I COULD COME BY IF I EVER HAD INGREDIENTS TO PUT ON THE HEARTH.
BUT WITH LORD BULL, I COULDN'T EVER KEEP ANY FOR MYSELF...
HE HAS AN ENCHANTED HAMMER THAT LETS HIM DO ANYTHING.
FROG. I HOPE YOU HAVE A GOOD REASON FOR BRINGING A MAMMAL HERE.

I AM CALLED YOSHI. IN RETURN FOR SOME RESPITE, I WILL GLADLY COOK IF YOU ALLOW ME TO FORAGE.
BEEN A WHILE SINCE A PROPER MEAL.
WE HAVE AN ABUNDANCE OF PICKLES AND A POND FULL OF FISH AS WELL.
I'M VERY GRATEFUL.
SIP.
A GREAT SPREAD!
HELP YOURSELVES! I INCLUDED A WESTERN-STYLE DISH TOO.

WESTERN FOOD?
I RUN A WESTERN-STYLE CAFE NEAR THE CITY.
THIS IS A "FISH TART".

THANKS FOR THE GRUB!
CITY MAMMALS AND THEIR STRANGE IDEAS. WE DON'T NEED... "TARTS".

REAL GOOD!
A FLAVOR I'VE NEVER HAD BEFORE!
BOING
HERE'S SOME FOR CHESTNUT.

NOT BAD. STILL, WHAT WE HAD BEFORE WAS JUST FINE.
AND HAD MORE JAPANESE SPIRIT!

CRASH
OUR FISH WERE PERSERVED IN RICE AND SALT, DUG UP IN TIME FOR THE YEARLY REED-BURNING...
IT WAS BEYOND COMPARE.

THE PICKLED FISH WAS SUPPOSED TO BE OUR RETIREMENT PLAN.

BUT WE RARELY SEE THE FRUITS OF OUR LABORS ANYMORE...
NOT WITH LORD BULL'S EVER FREQUENT TRIBUTES.

I HEARD HE USED TO BE A PRIZE BULL FOR HUMANS BACK IN THE OLD DAYS.
HUMANS DROVE HIM AWAY WHEN THEY WANTED TO IMPRESS THE FOREIGNERS. GAVE HIM THAT HAMMER.
THEY SAID THERE'S NO ROOM FOR MAGIC BEASTS.

A SAD STORY. BUT WE CAN'T GO ON LIKE THIS. SOMETHING HAS TO CHANGE.

I THINK I MAY HAVE A WAY TO REASON WITH LORD BULL.
I JUST NEED TO DELIVER THIS PACKAGE.

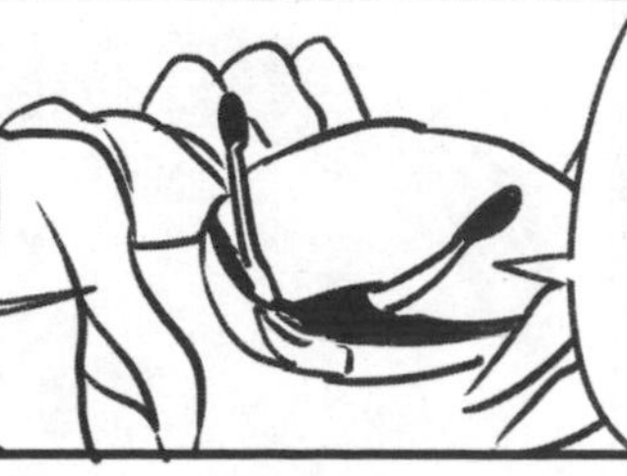
YOU REMIND ME OF MYSELF WHEN I WAS YOUNGER.
A BATTLE WITH A TYRANNICAL MONKEY. IT'S HOW I MET CHESTNUT.

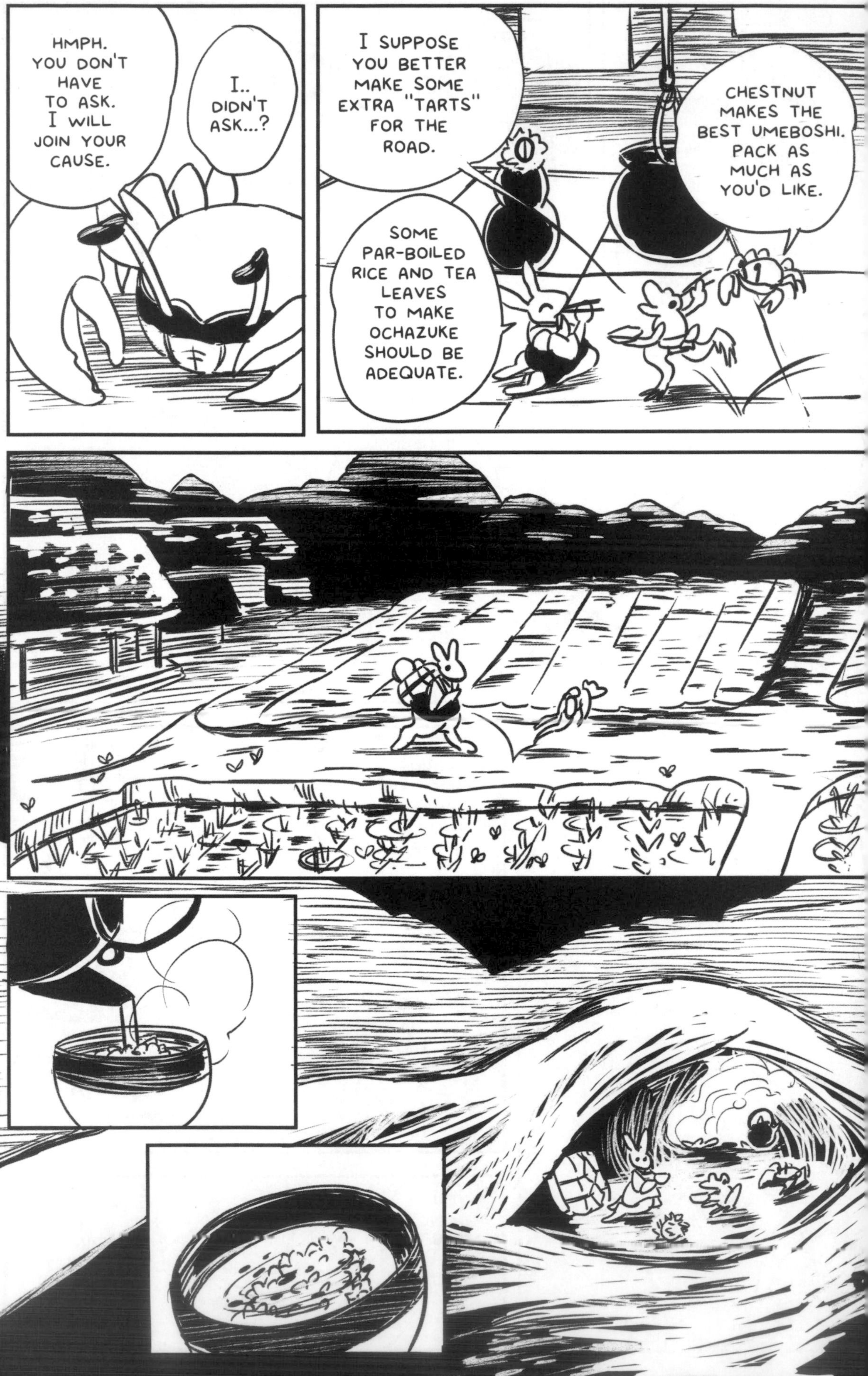

HMPH. YOU DON'T HAVE TO ASK. I WILL JOIN YOUR CAUSE.
I.. DIDN'T ASK...?
I SUPPOSE YOU BETTER MAKE SOME EXTRA "TARTS" FOR THE ROAD.
CHESTNUT MAKES THE BEST UMEBOSHI. PACK AS MUCH AS YOU'D LIKE.
SOME PAR-BOILED RICE AND TEA LEAVES TO MAKE OCHAZUKE SHOULD BE ADEQUATE.

FOR YOUR TROUBLES. CAN YOU TELL US WHERE THE FIRE REEDS ARE?
CLOSE BY, NO DOUBT! YOU'RE ON THE RIGHT TRACK! MUCH OBLIGED ON THE GRUB, HA!

I-I OF COURSE WOULD TAKE THIS STRAIGHT AWAY TO LORD BULL, OK!
I-I HAVE MORE THAN ENOUGH, HEH! HE ALWAYS PROVIDES!

FFLIKT!
N-NEVER HAVE TO W-WORRY--

THAT SMELL...

A MAGNIFICENT AND DREADFUL FIRE...
I'VE NEVER SEEN IT IN PERSON.

!!

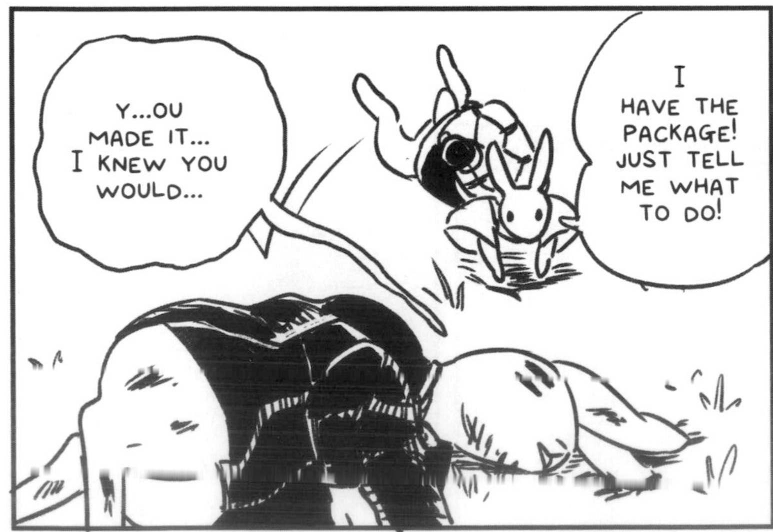
Y...OU MADE IT... I KNEW YOU WOULD...
I HAVE THE PACKAGE! JUST TELL ME WHAT TO DO!

ANOTHER TRIBUTE?

THE HUMANS MUST HAVE SENT YOU...
...TO APOLOGIZE FOR BANISHING ME.
THE PACKAGE-- THERE'S ARMOR INSIDE.
TAKE MY SWORD AND END THIS.
A-AREN'T THESE CONTRABAND!?
SNIP
LORD BULL IS BEYOND REASONING... THE HUMANS, I'VE NO IDEA WHAT THEY'VE DONE...
...BUT THERE IS NO PLACE FOR A BEAST LIKE HIM IN THIS NEW WORLD...

HUP
FROG! DAZE HIM WITH YOUR STRENGTH!
PAP
PAP
RIGHT-O!
HUP
CRAB, SEE IF YOU CAN THROW HIM OFF BALANCE!
JUST LIKE OLD TIMES, EH, GIRL?
CHESTNUT, YOU KNOW WHAT TO DO!
FWIP
FWOOOM

BAM!
TSING
TSING!
SLAM!
HUFF
HUFF...

DON'T WORRY, IT'LL BE OKAY!
I HAD A DREAM ABOUT YOU!
HEH...
Y'KNOW...
I HAD A DREAM ABOUT YOU, TOO...
SHINK

YOU... HAVE BETRAYED THE OLD WAYS...
WE WILL BUILD A NEW WORLD BASED ON LESSONS WE LEARNED FROM THE OLD WORLD.
BUT WE CAN'T SURVIVE IF YOU'RE HOLDING US BACK!
SWISH...
I RELEASE YOU INTO THE REEDS!

WE'VE COME A LONG WAY TO FINISH WHAT YOU STARTED.
AND WE HAVE A LONG WAY YET TO GO.
THE END.

TRACK
EVAN DAHM

YES
YES THE TRACK
THIS,
THIS, YES
THE TRACK THE
THE TRACK
TRAC
YES

NO NO NO NO NO NO NO
ILL PLACE BAD BAD BAD PLACE
DEATH DEATH
NO PLACE
NO NO BAD PLACE
NO NO NO NO
NO THE TRACK!
NO?
N NO?

ILL
ILL
PLACE
NO
NO
NO
NO
NONO NO
THIS THIS THIS THE TRACK
THI.
THIS?
THIS
THIS?
THIS
NO
THI
TH
THIS?
NO
NO
NO

THI
TH
NN NO
MNO
NO
NO
EVIL
NO
ILL
PLACE
NO
ILL
OOD
RICH
GOOD
PLACE
GOOD
TH T THIS TH

GOOD
THIS
GOOD
GOOD
RICH
RI
RICH
THI
THIS PLACE

NO
NO
NO
NO
NO
NO
NO
NO NO NO
NO
NO
NO
NO
NO

NO
NO
NONO
NO
NO
TH TH
THIS?
THIS
THIS?

WH
THIS
WHAT
THIS
TH
THIS
PLACE
THIS
YES
Y
TH

YES
Y
THIS
GOOD
GOOD RICH PLACE

TH'
THIS
NO N
NO
N
EVIL
NO
TH
THIS NO
NO NO
WH WHAT
WHAT
THIS

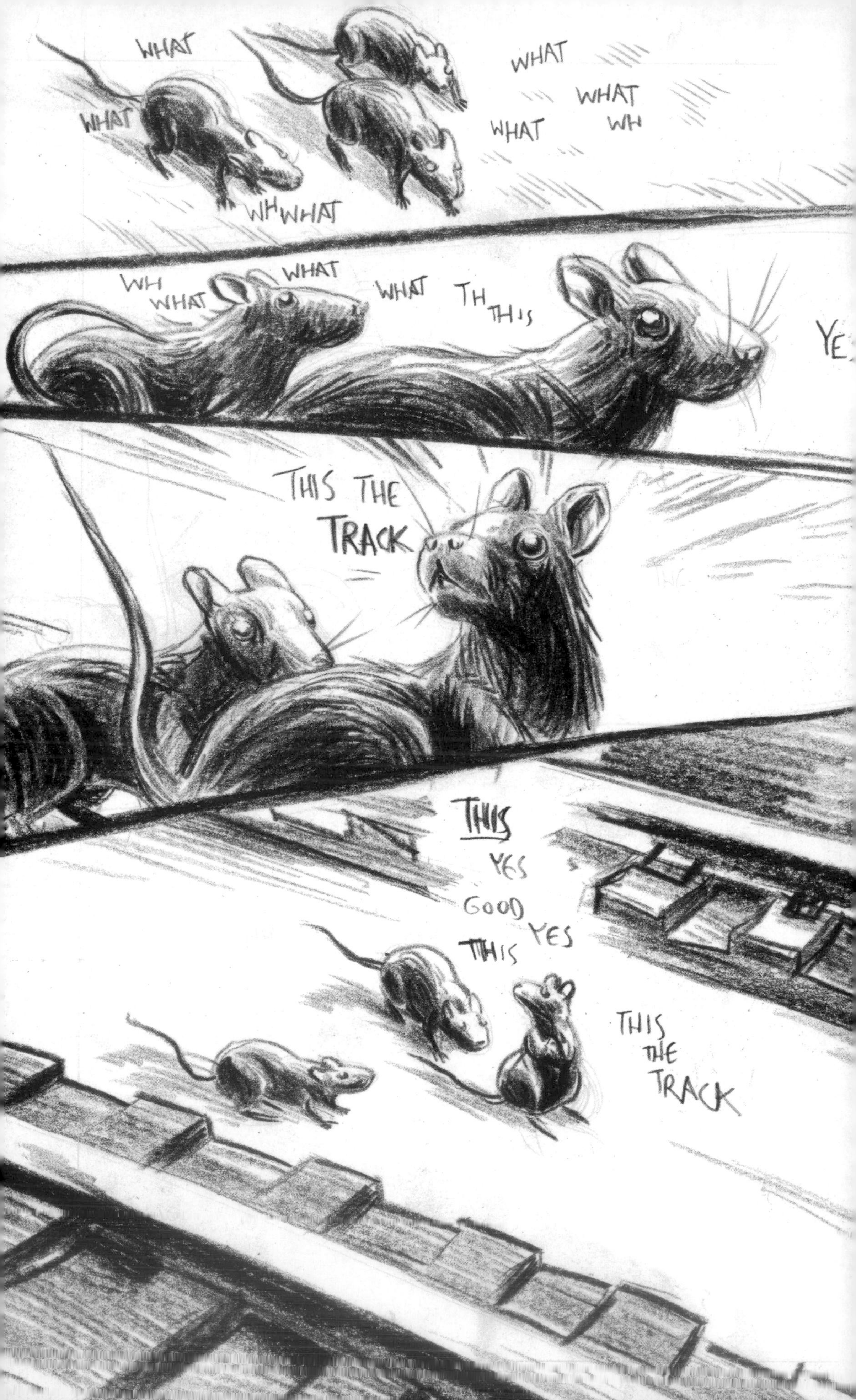
WHAT
WHAT
WHAT
WHAT
WHAT
WHAT WH
WH WHAT
WH WHAT
WHAT
WHAT
TH THIS
YE
THIS THE TRACK
THIS
YES
GOOD
YES
THIS
THIS THE TRACK

TH
THIS
THIS
THIS
YES
THE TRACK

THE LONG BRIDGE
Jessi Zabarsky

Who
is THAT?

Well, she's so popular.

Y'know, she's strong, and gentle, so everyone likes her.

But she's never had a mate, or even a kiss-friend.

Her island is just so far away from the rest of us.

KIMIT

Yeesh, you've got it bad, huh?

You should go to the Conna, I think.

'One who
wishes to make
a permanent
connection with
another must
make that wish
tangible.'

'She must build
a bridge from her
home to her love's,
and hope that,
once it is completed,
her love will
accept her offer
by joining her on
the bridge.'

'She must build the
bridge all of
her own hand.
The bridge must
be strong enough
to support the
town,
as none of us,
single or coupled,
can stand alone.'

Hurrah!
You can do it!
Kimit!

PLONK

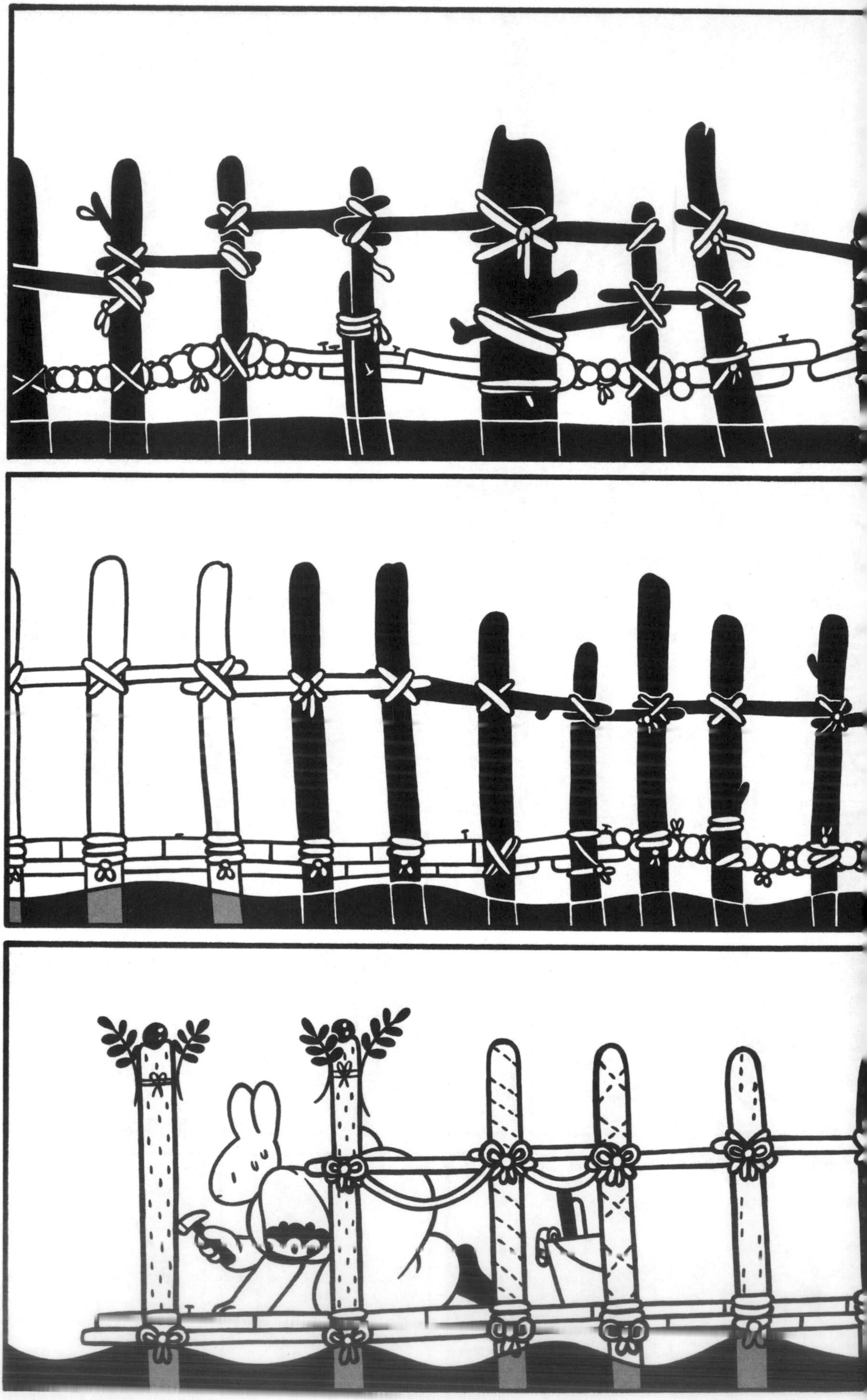

halloooooo

Please, get in, I'll row you to shore!
It's too dangerous!

Don't fret, I'll be fine!
Get on home!

AAAAAA

Kimit?

Oh! You're awake!
Good, I've got soup.

Come now, you have to get your strength back!
I shouldn't-
I can't-
I have no right-
I failed.
Let me show you something.

But still...
I didn't...
Had you not been so determined-
Had you not fallen-
Had I not so feared for you-
I could not have completed it.
This is still your bridge.

HOO
RAY!

Then, it could be our bridge, if you would have me.

KIMIT!
REKA!

FROG AND TOAD.

SO CLOSE ARE OUR TWO SPECIES THAT AT A GLANCE WE MAY BE MISTAKEN FOR THE SAME, AND YET STILL WE CROSS BLADES.

WHERE ONCE WE GATHERED AS BROTHERS AND SISTERS IN FRIENDLY COMPETITION, DESPERATION NOW GUIDES OUR HANDS.

WITH THE ZEAL OF THOSE WHO HAVE GONE WITHOUT.

WE FIGHT BECAUSE WE MUST...

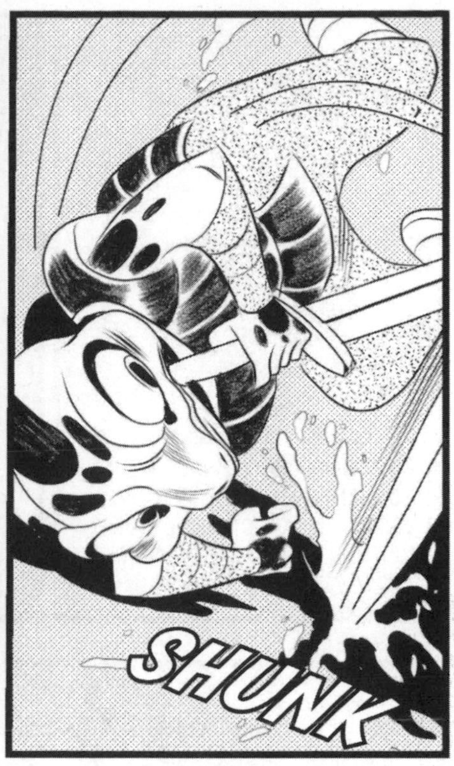

THEY HARDLY EVEN WATCH THE SPECTACLE THEY DEMAND OF US, THEIR REVELS A BACKDROP TO SHED BLOOD AND BROKEN BONES.

RAINMAKER

STORY: GAVIN FALCON · ART: ANNA WIESZCZYK · LETTERS: CLAUDIA CANGINI

BUT WHAT CHOICE HAVE WE, US LOW AND MISERLY CREATURES, WHEN SELF-APPOINTED LEADERS CONTROL THE MEANS OF OUR SURVIVAL?

CLANG

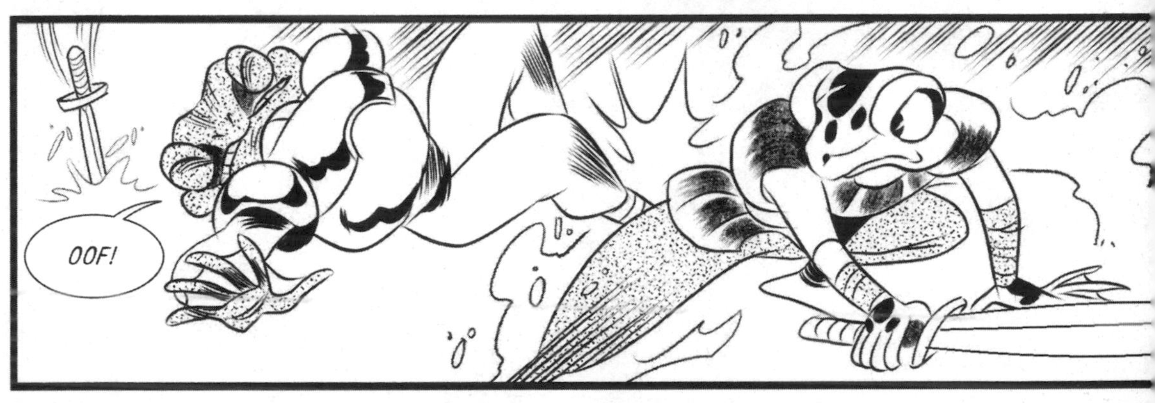
OOF!

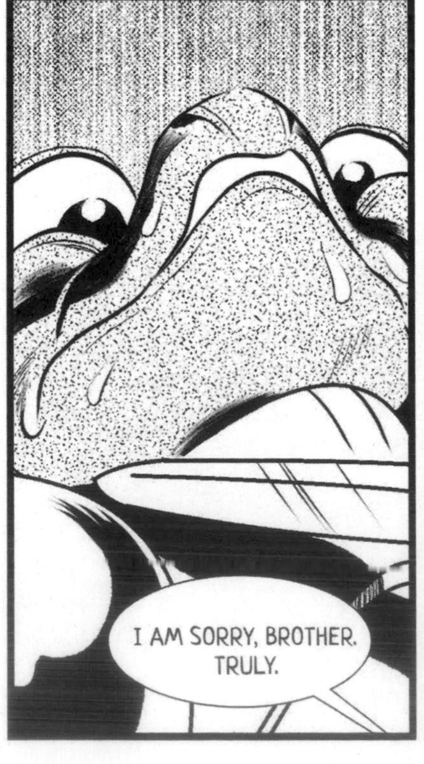
I AM SORRY, BROTHER. TRULY.

THE DRY SLUMS. THESE STREETS HAVE NOT TASTED WATER REGULARLY FOR YEARS. THE YOUNG AND NAIVE SUSPECT A CURSE...

BUT SOME OF US KNOW BETTER.

STOP, PLEASE!
THE MICE FANCY THEMSELVES LORDS OF WEATHER, DEMANDING TITHE AND SUBSERVIENCE IN EXCHANGE FOR PRODUCING THE WATER WE SO DESPERATELY NEED.

FOR YEARS, EVER SINCE THE RAINS STOPPED FALLING, WE SUFFERED THEM HAPPILY FOR FEAR OF THE ALTERNATIVE.

BUT AS TIME WENT BY, THE RAINS CAME FURTHER AND FURTHER APART, AND THE DEMANDS GREW MORE EXTREME.
TAKE ME! TAKE ME INSTEAD!

FIRST CAME THE GLADIATORIAL COMBAT BETWEEN US AND THE TOADS, WITH THE PROMISE THAT THE VICTORS WOULD EARN THEIR PEOPLE THE FAVOR OF THE GODS.

NO!
NOW THEY DEMAND BLOOD, CLAIMING WITH TWISTED GRINS THAT IT APPEASES THE DEITIES THEY SO RIGHTEOUSLY SERVE.

THE TIME TO ABIDE HAS GONE.

IT HAS SINCE BECOME A LOOMING REMINDER OF THE MICE'S POWER.

YOU MANAGE TO MAKE IT OVER TO THE FIGHT PIT EARLIER? TOADS BROUGHT HOME A WIN AGAIN!
YEAH, I'M ALMOST STARTIN' TO FEEL BAD FOR THEM FROGS MYSELF. STOPPED TO GRAB A DRINK AT ONE OF THEIR BARS AFTERWARDS AND THE WATER COST MORE THAN THE SWILL!

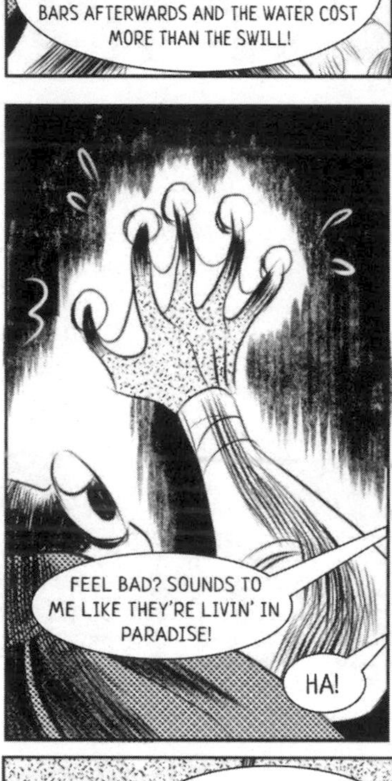
FEEL BAD? SOUNDS TO ME LIKE THEY'RE LIVIN' IN PARADISE!
HA!

WITHOUT ESCORT. VIOLATORS AND THEIR FAMILIES WILL BE EXECUTED

HEY, YOU HEAR SOMETHING TOO?
CLNK

YEAH, PROBABLY JUST THOSE DAMN BATS DROPPING CRAP ON US AGAIN. IT NEVER STOPS WITH THEM, I SWEAR.

TOAD TERRITORY. FAR AS I'M AWARE, NONE OF MY PEOPLE HAVE TRAVERSED THIS SIDE OF THE WALL IN NEARLY A DECADE.

I ONLY HOPE THEY ARE SENSITIVE TO OUR PLIGHT, PROVIDED I CAN EVEN FIND THEM IN THIS SPRAWL.

FOLLOWING THE FLOW OF THE FOREST SEEMS THE BEST OPTION, GIVEN THE CIRCUMSTANCE.

STREAMS, LIKE ROADS, ALWAYS LEAD TO SOMEWHERE AFTER ALL.

WELL, WHAT DO WE HAVE HERE?

SO HERE IS THE INTERLOPER,
WHO SOUGHT TO INTRUDE UPON OUR
HOMES AND LIVES. WHY IS IT YOU HAVE
COME HERE, FROG?

WERE THE RULES SET BY YOUR BETTERS NOT CLEAR? THE PENALTIES NOT DIRE ENOUGH TO DISSUADE YOU FROM BREAKING THEM?
OR ARE YOU SIMPLY INDIFFERENT?

SIR, PLEASE. I HAVE NOT COME TO INVADE, BUT TO HUMBLY ASK YOUR ASSISTANCE. FOR YEARS MY PEOPLE HAVE BEEN LOCKED IN A STATE OF DROUGHT, PERPETUATED BY THE MICE WHO FORCED US APART SO LONG AGO.
WORSE, THEY HAVE BEGUN DEMANDING RITUAL SACRIFICE, SLAUGHTERING US FOR PROMISE OF RAIN THAT WON'T COME. WILL YOU HELP ME TAKE UP ARMS AGAINST THEM, IN THE NAME OF RESTORING TIES AND REMOVING OUR COLLECTIVE OPPRESSORS?
YOU ARE PROPOSING THAT WE, WHO HOLD THE GOD'S FAVOR, FORSAKE IT TO MARCH AGAINST THE VERY SAME WHO HAVE GIVEN US SUCH PROSPERITY? TO THROW AWAY ALL THAT WE HAVE WORKED TO ACHIEVE, FOR THE SAKE OF *YOUR* PEOPLE? ESTEEMED MEMBERS OF THE COUNCIL, WHAT SAY YOU?
KILL HIM!
LOCK HIM UP!
HAND HIM OVER TO THE MICE!
GUARDS, LET THIS FROG ROT IN THE PRISON UNTIL WE DECIDE WHAT TO DO WITH HIM.

LATER...
COME TO DELIVER THE VERDICT OF MY GRUESOME DEMISE?
CREEEK
NOT HARDLY. IN FACT, I'VE COME TO RELEASE YOU.

CHNK
LISTEN CAREFULLY: YOU MUST ESCAPE THE CITY, CLIMB INTO THE SKY AND TALK TO THE CREATURES THERE. THEY MAY NEED CONVINCING, BUT WILL GIVE YOU THE AID YOU SEEK.

WELL? DO YOU PLAN TO SIT THERE ALL NIGHT, OR ARE YOU GOING TO GET MOVING?

WHY ARE YOU HELPING ME?
WE HAVE NOT ALL HAD THE VEIL PULLED OVER OUR EYES, YOUNG ONE. NOW, YOU WILL BE HARD PRESSED TO NAVIGATE OUR LAND ON YOUR OWN, SO I HAVE ENLISTED A GUIDE.

HELLO AGAIN. IT IS GOOD TO FINALLY MEET YOU WITHOUT NEEDING TO CROSS BLADES.

SPEAKING OF, I BELIEVE THIS IS YOURS.

HERE, USE THESE TO COVER YOUR FACE AND HANDS UNTIL WE'RE OUT OF THE CITY.

THERE HE IS!

THE PEOPLE'S CHAMPION! KEEPING THE WATER FLOWING! CONGRATULATIONS ON ANOTHER BIG WIN, YOU WERE SPECTACULAR.
OH, UH, THANK YOU SO MUCH.

WHO'S THAT WITH YOU THERE, ANOTHER FAN?
JUST A FRIEND FROM THE FIGHT PITS. GOT CUT UP PRETTY BAD IN HIS LAST BOUT, SO HE'S TRYING TO KEEP THE WOUNDS COVERED.
OUCH, SORRY TO HEAR IT.

BUT HEY, AT LEAST WE CAME OUT ON TOP AGAIN. I MEAN, BETTER THEM THAN US, YEAH?
SURE, RIGHT...

I'M CURIOUS ABOUT SOMETHING, IF YOU WOULD CARE TO ENLIGHTEN ME.
I'LL CERTAINLY TRY MY BEST.
IT'S A LIMITED OBSERVATION, BUT YOUR PEOPLE SEEM HAPPY AND YOUR CITY BORDERS ON IDEAL.
AND YOU WISH TO KNOW ON WHAT GROUNDS I STAND AGAINST THIS, CORRECT?

WELL, YES.
I SIMPLY ASKED MYSELF WHAT MANNER OF GODS WOULD BOAST OF COMPASSION FOR ALL AND SCORN A PORTION OF THOSE THEY CLAIM DOMINION OVER IN THE SAME BREATH, AND THE ANSWER WAS PLAIN...

FALSE GODS.

A SHAME THAT MORE CAN'T REACH THE SAME CONCLUSION.
I THINK YOU WOULD BE SURPRISED.

OH? THEN WHY ARE THERE NOT MORE HERE BY OUR SIDES TO HELP HALT THE MOUSE REGIME?
FEAR IS A POWERFUL DETERRENT, MY FRIEND; ESPECIALLY FEAR FOR ONE'S LIFE. FEW ARE THOSE THAT HAVE STRENGTH ENOUGH TO TAKE THE FIRST STEP SO OTHERS MAY FOLLOW BEHIND.

TRUE THAT MAY BE, BUT--
FWOOOSH
WHAT WAS THAT?

REEEEEEE

THIS IS NO PLACE FOR YOU, WINGLESS CREATURES. WHY HAVE YOU COME TO SUCH GREAT HEIGHTS?
THEY'RE ON SOME SORTA MISSION AGAINST THOSE MICE, I HEARD 'EM SAY IT MYSELF!

IS THIS TRUE?
IT IS. WE COME SEEKING WHATEVER HELP YOU CAN SPARE RETURNING THE RAINS TO MY PEOPLE.

I SEE... THEN PERHAPS WE CAN AID ONE ANOTHER IN EQUAL MEASURE.
HOW?

WE WILL TAKE YOU THERE, TRAVELERS...

BUT WHAT ELSE LURKS INSIDE
IS A MYSTERY EVEN TO US.

FLY FAST AND FLY
LOW. WE WILL KEEP WATCH
FROM ABOVE.

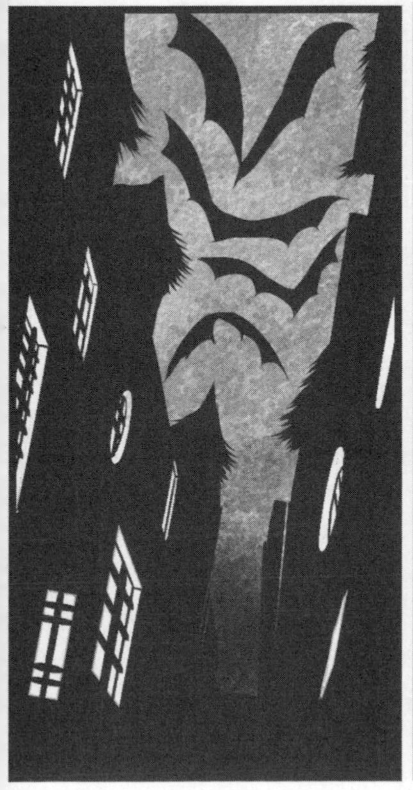

SNRKT~*

ANY IDEAS ON WHAT THIS "KEY" MIGHT BE?

I'M NOT ONE FOR GUESSWORK...

BUT I THINK WE MAY HAVE ALREADY FOUND IT.

UY! WHUT'S THAT NOISE!?

I CAN HOLD THEM OFF,
GO!

OOF!

REEEEEE
THAT HALLWAY WAS A TIGHT FIT. HAD TO LEAVE THE OTHERS BEHIND!

NEVER THOUGHT I'D BE SO GLAD TO BE THE RUNT! NOW, GO HELP YOUR FRIEND!

CHNK
HOIST ME UP!

CHNK

IT'S UP TO YOU NOW, MY FRIEND.

ZZZZZZT

END.

It was mother taught me how to hunt.
Catch the scent.
Chase.
Quarry's faster than us, but we hem it in. Force it back to the burrow.
Track it home. Claws in dirt. Dig down. Flush it out.
Shake 'till it snaps.
Now the family can eat.
Myths of the Wild Bassets
Graham Overby

But those are the good hunts.
In winter, futile hunts are many. There is never enough.

Last winter, Mother's hind legs gave out. Could drag herself a span, but never would run again.

We all brought food, little we could find.

But she told us,
"Better to feed your pups. Grow them up big and strong like you."

So we did. My nieces and nephews did not go hungry. That season was so long.

Before first thaw, Mother died.

I said nothing for the rest of winter. But when spring came, I told my kin,

They came
with me, at first.
Mother used to tell about a
Black Path on forest's edge, leads
to the mountain where the Allfathers rest.
We followed the setting sun till we found
it, running snake-like through the wood.

"The monster."

"'A horror that guards the Allfathers' den...'"
"Just as Mother told it!"
"So the monster is real... We must turn back."

"I'm sorry. I wanted you to find your answers. I did."

"No. The monster doesn't scare me. I am going into the mountain."
"Wait-"
"Please-"
"Auntie!"
"I'll bring back word from the All-fathers. I promise."

Walked in the dark till I lost a feel for time. Hardly believed when I saw, round a corner, dim light.
And there I found...
You.
CAT!!
You fled--I couldn't help but chase.
"Wait till I tell them their 'monster' is a cat!"
"I'll be 'the hound who slew the horror!'"
Deeper, deeper, deeper into the mountain--no scent to track, but I followed.
Thought I had you cornered, when--

"Well met, good hound! Thank you for the chase! It was exhilarating!"
To my surprise, you spoke!
You offered to guide me to the Allfathers, provided--
Yes, provided you tell me how it was you came here. I was there for that part, silly dog.
Then it's all told.
And quite well. Thank you.
I'm sorry for your loss.
Please... Please take me to the Allfathers.
Of course.
SHHFF
Follow me.

We've still some ways to go. Perhaps there's more you might tell me. Of the Allfathers, say.
You live in their den--don't you know already?
I want to hear *your* version, if you wouldn't mind.
So it's true about curiosity and cats... Fine: the Allfathers...
The Allfathers created dogs. They lived with us a long time ago.
We hunted with them--but only for the joy of the hunt. They had enough food for everyone.
They created spaces, like here. But then their spaces were full of light. Warm in the cold, cool in the heat.

There came a time when the Allfathers grew tired. They went to sleep here, under this mountain.
But someday will come a spring that lasts forever, when the Allfathers will wake.
Yet you intend to awaken them now?
Not for long-- huff need to ask them-- questions. Important questions.
You... seem a bit winded. Are you entirely sure you'll be able to make it all the way back up when your audience is finished? Perhaps you should turn back now.
Just out of breath from too much talking. No turning back.
As I see it, *you're* the curious one, coming all this way just to ask a few questions.

Behind this door lies the Allfathers' chamber. I have fulfilled my obligation.
Cat. I owe you more than I can say.
I will not stop you if you wish to proceed. But are you cert-
Don't.
Everyone's tried to tell me why I can't, or won't make it there, won't make it back.
None of them... understand why I came here.
That's not what I'm saying. You made it. You're here. You've nothing to prove.
What I am asking is: have you considered you might be happier without seeing the Allfathers?
That there are things better not known?
This was never about proving.
I need to talk to them.
Open the door. Please.

rrr
rrrrr
grrrr
RRRR

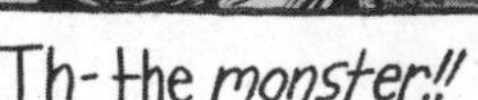
Th-the *monster!!*

RUN, you fool!!

GRRRRRRR
RAAAAA
ZZZZZ
VOIP
!?

ZZZZZZzzt--

I suppose I should have known that wouldn't work.

There is no monster. Only me --
The Allfather's caretaker.
Cat? Where are you? Where's the monster?

I... I don't understand...

In these vaults, I can fashion illusions -- a monster, or a cat --
Cat!!
CHK

--but they aren't real. You see, I have no body, just metal that houses me. I can't leave this place.
ZZZ

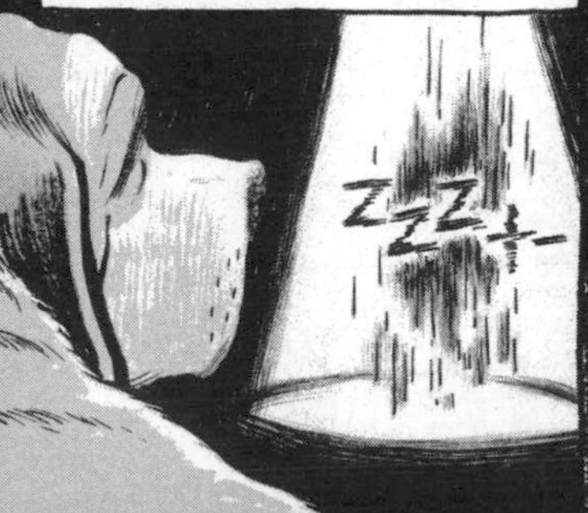

I don't understand.
CHK

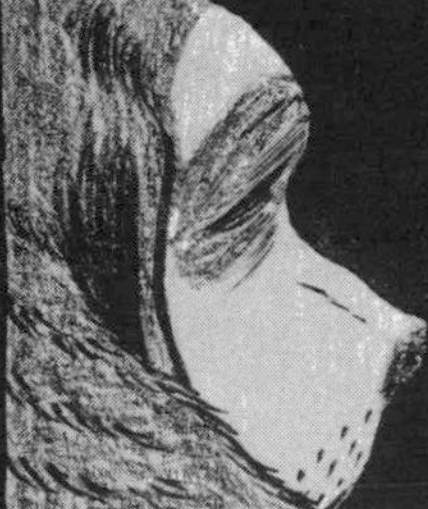
I'm sorry I tricked you. I only wanted to play.
But I suppose now I owe you the full truth, as best I know it...

Let me tell you a story about a time when the Allfathers covered the whole world: as you said, they brought light, and food, and warmth in the winter, and coolness in the summer.
But these things they brought unbalanced the world. It became too hot, or too cold, or too wet or too dry to live.
The Allfathers tried to restore the proper order, with their tools that changed the air and plants and animals. They were very clever with tools.
Yet the more the Allfathers tried to fix their mistakes, the worse they became. For you see, though they understood and controlled many things, the workings of the world were too complex even for them.
They brought terrible sicknesses. The animals were dying, the Allfathers too. Some survived: by chance, by their makeup, they were immune. Such as your kind. But not the Allfathers themselves.
They stopped trying to fix their mistakes, and saw they could not live in this world without hurting it.
So they made a new one. With their tools of metal and lightning, they made another world, like a dream, and escaped into it.
They left me behind to keep their dream-world safe.

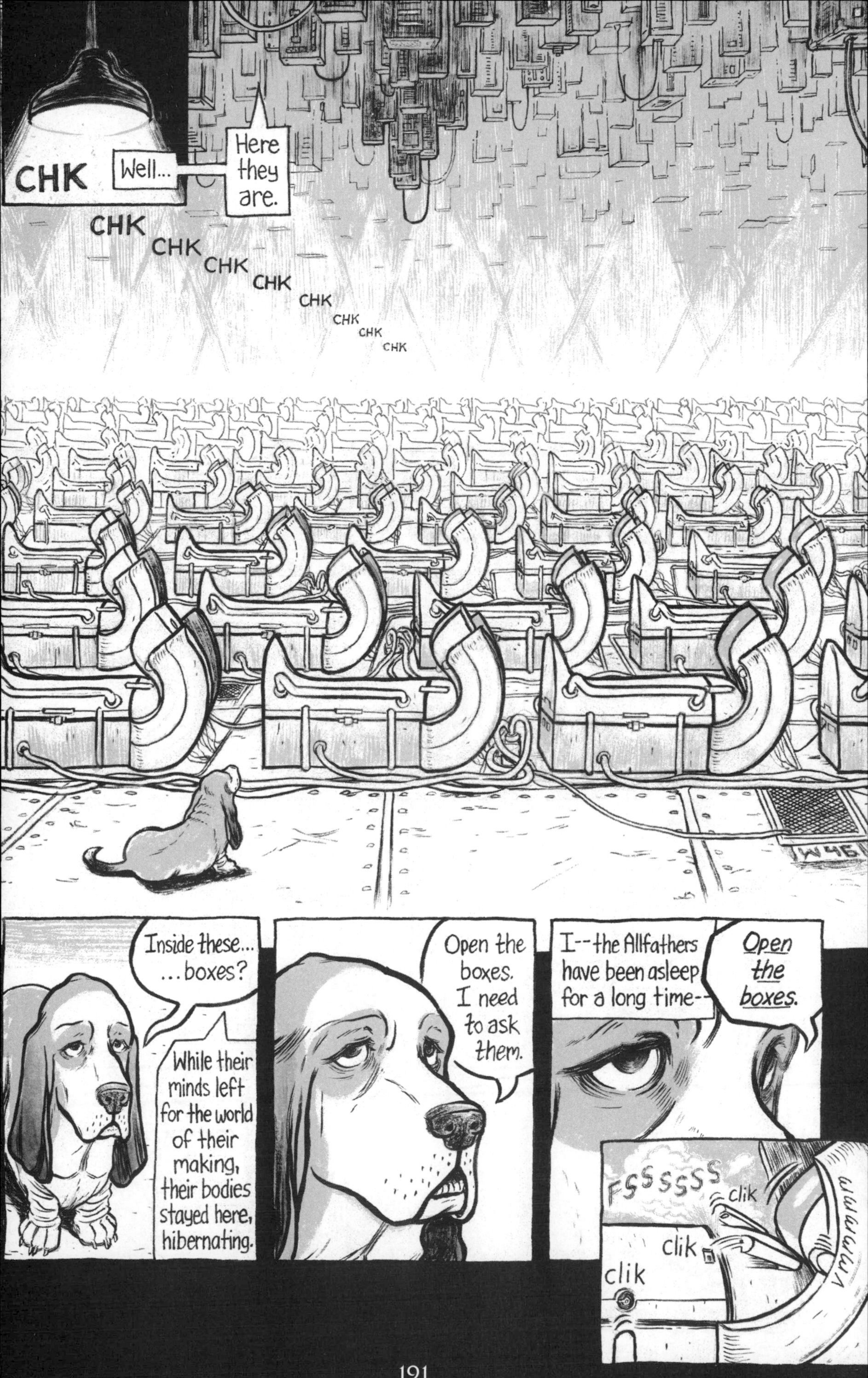
CHK
Well...
Here they are.
CHK
CHK
CHK
CHK
CHK
CHK
CHK
CHK
W46
Inside these... ...boxes?
While their minds left for the world of their making, their bodies stayed here, hibernating.
Open the boxes. I need to ask them.
I--the Allfathers have been asleep for a long time--
Open the boxes.
FSSSSSS
clik
clik
clik

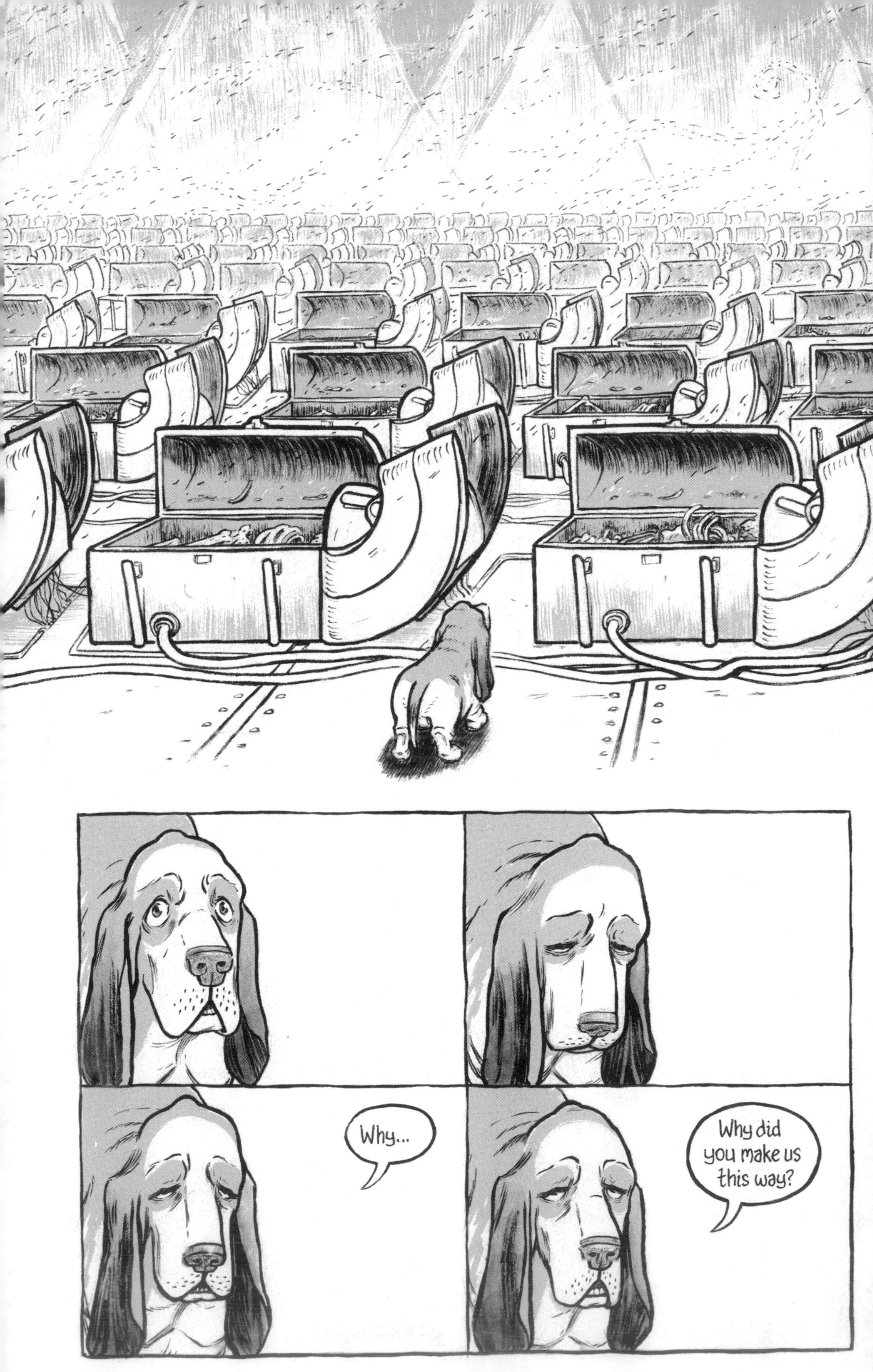
Why...
Why did you make us this way?

So slow we never catch our quarries?

So weak we barely pierce their hides?

Why is the winter so long and food so scarce??

Why -- why must we die --

as my Mother died --

dragging ourselves forward on two legs??

Why?

WHY??

WH--WOOOOOOOOOOOOOOOOOOOOOO
I could... try to answer your questions. If you'd like.
--
I should have told you the truth about the Allfathers when we first met.
But I judged you happier not knowing. And I so enjoyed walking with you.
Listen...
The Allfathers made your legs short so they could keep pace with you on foot. To hunt alongside you, for your noses were better than theirs.
They made your jaws weak so they could keep your catches as trophies. For they would feed you from their tables.
They never intended for you to survive without them. To outlast them.
Were we... tools, to the Allfathers?
Perhaps you were created as tools, but you were loved.
They hunted and lived with you, and loved you.

Are you going to leave now?
I... I don't know.
CHK
If you sleep here, I can take your mind out of your body. Like them.
!
ZZZZZZK
Can I go where the Allfathers are?
No. Their world is closed. But you could stay here, with me.
Stay...?
As I said, the Allfathers created me to ensure their slumber would not be interrupted.
They made it so I could learn -- so I could adapt to whatever might threaten their dream-world in the future.
I learned to be lonely. They didn't know I would do that.
If you stay here, you can tell me more of the world outside, the one I can never reach. And I can tell you more about the Allfathers.
You will not have to hunt and scavenge through the scarcity of winter, and you will never die.
Will you stay?

I would...
I would like to stay.
But...
My pack. I told my pack I would bring word.
Do you really think they should know what you found here?
Why? Why return to that world?
I...
...The Allfathers left us. Left them.
I won't.
Commendable.
But, consider: you have come a long way.
You are tired, and thirsty.
The stairs will be harder to climb than they were to descend.
Do you believe you will be able to go up the way you came down?
I will try.
Even if I am to die on the stairs.

Never have I met such a steadfast creature...Ah, well.
I wouldn't let you perish, not here in my home. Nor, I suppose, would I have kept you under false pretenses, much as I might want to.
Over here.
!
Come in--
this room will take you back to the surface.
SHH
HFF
Cat!
ZZZZZZ

"I tread deep into the dark vaults, outwalking any measure of distance.
"I saw the Allfathers' beds, now empty.
"I faced the monster, but it was no monster at all, just a lonely ghost in the Allfathers' machines.
"It told me this: the Allfathers made us wit short legs to hunt alongside us, just as they lived alongside us, and loved us
"It told me the Allfathers delivered us from the sickness that scoured the other animals.
"It told me they saved our world, by leaving for another one.
"Someday may come a spring that brings them back."
Ahh... It's a good story.

THE TADPOLE TWINS...

...ARE FLIPPERS DOWN, THE **BEST** FIGHTERS IN THE POND!

YEAH, 'CAUSE THEY HATCHED FROM THE **SAME** EGG!

THEY'VE BEEN FIGHTING SINCE **BEFORE** THEY HATCHED!

THE TADPOLE TWINS VERSUS BUREAUCRACY

David McGuire

CAN YOU TADS TELL ME HOW TO FIND...
...WHAT'D YOU SAY THEIR NAMES WERE AGAIN?
CINNAMON AND MINT!
THEY'RE FIGHTING A SALAMANDER!
BEHIND YOU!
STAY STILL YOU POLLYWOGS, SO I CAN CUT YOU!
STOMP!
CHOMP!
FWAP FWAP FWAP
BOOT!
HEADBUTT COMBO

I GIVE!
I GIVE!
UNCLE!
...
THAT'S MINE.
!!
YOU NEXT, MISTER?
BAP
NEXT FOR WHAT?
PEOPLE COME FROM ALL OVER TO FIGHT US!
MY SISTER AND I SEEM TO'VE DEVELOPED A REPUTATION.

EASY, TADS.
I'M A PENCIL PUSHER, NOT A FIGHTING FROG.

I'M NUTCAP SWAMPKIN.
CINNAMON AND MINT, RIGHT?
DOFF
YEAH.

THE FROG COUNCIL SENT ME HERE.
WHO?

JOIN ME IN MY OFFICE UP T AND I'LL EXPLA EVERYTHING.

• • •

SURE.

OH, YOU TWO DO HAVE LUNGS BY NOW, RIGHT?

TOPSIDE OF THE OL' POND

CENSUS OFFICE

ANYWAY, THE POND YOU'RE CURRENTLY GROWING UP IN IS THE FROG SOCIETY'S NURSERY. OUR BREEDING "GROUNDS" IF YOU WILL.

UNFORTUNATELY, THIS PLACE IS ***INFESTED*** WITH FISH.

WITH ENOUGH EGGS, WE ENSURE AT LEAST A FEW FROGS SURVIVE.

BUT YOU TWO HAVE THROWN A WRENCH INTO THE WORKS!

OKAY...
SO.
WHAT'S--
WHAT'S A WRENCH?
YEAH.

BECAUSE YOU TWO BEAT UP SO MANY FISH, THEY'RE AFRAID TO EAT ANY TADPOLES.

AND THAT'S...
BAD?

EXACTLY!

I DON'T--
BECAUSE WE LAY SO MANY EGGS!

YOUR WELL-INTENTIONED **MEDDLING** IS LEADING TO A POPULATION **EXPLOSION**, WRECKING THE **ECOLOGY**.

DID YOU KNOW THE AVERAGE FROG CAN LAY UP TO **TWENTY-THOUSAND EGGS** A YEAR?

WATER WE **SUSTOADS** TO DO? LET OUR FRIENDS BECOME **FISH FOOD?**

YES!
THANK YOU!
I **TOLD** THE FROG COUNCIL YOU'D UNDERSTAND!

NO TADPOLE'S **CROAKING** ON OUR WATCH, NUTCAP.
GO CROSS A ROAD.

OH FROG.
I REALLY HOPED I COULD TALK SOME SENSE INTO YOU.

WELL, JOIN ME OUTSIDE FOR THE FROG COUNCIL'S SOLUTION.
SORRY I HAVE TO DO THIS, BUT RULES ARE RULES.
?
?

ALRIGHT, PERCY.
MY WAY FAILED.
HERE'S THE INVASIVE SPECIES.
DO YOUR THING.
!
CENSUS OFFICE

WHOA WHOA WHOA
WATER YOU TRYING TO PULL, SWAMPKIN?
HUH?

"HUH," HE SAYS!

LOOK HOW **BRIGHTLY COLORED** THEY ARE!
THOSE FROG BABIES'RE **OBVIOUSLY** POISONOUS!

PROBABLY NOT? THEY'RE VERY SMALL. I'M SURE IT'S OKAY.

I'M EATING **YOU** INSTEAD.

GOBBLE
GOBBLE

SHOULD WE RESCUE HIM?
YEAH, OF COURSE!

HE TRIED TO FEED US TO THAT THING.
YEAH, BUT I'VE ALWAYS WANTED TO FIGHT AN ALLIGATOR!

?
kick
kick

WHAP!
CHEW
CHE

CINNAMON! WE'RE OUT OF OUR ELEMENT!

YOU MEAN WATER?
YEAH, WE CAN'T BEAT HIM ON LAND!

HEY! LET'S JUMP IN HIS MOUTH!
WHAT.

HE THINKS WE'RE POISONOUS, RIGHT?
...

RUN!
RUN!
RUN!

SERIOUSLY?
ARE THOSE KIDS SERIOUSLY STILL TRYING TO--

ZIP!

OH NO!

WHAT EXACTLY WAS YOUR PLAN HERE?

UM...
WE'RE PLAYING IT BY EAR.
FROGS DON'T HAVE EARS!

HACK
HACK
HACK
HACK
BARF!
URP
OH FROG, WE'RE ALIVE!!
YOU TADS ARE MY HEROES!
I'LL NEVER BE ABLE TO REPAY YOU ENOUGH!

YOU KNOW WHAT?
I **RENOUNCE** THE FROG COUNCIL! YOU TADS ARE ***THE FUTURE!***

I'LL DO EVERYTHING I CAN TO ENSURE YOUR GENERATION DOESN'T HAVE TO PAY FOR THE MISTAKES OF MY GENERATION!

OH, COOL. WELL, THANKS!
AND IF YOU EVER NEED A FAVOR, LET ME KNOW!

HEY, THE ONLY THING *I* NEED AFTER THAT EXPERIENCE IS A ***BATH!***

HA HA HA HA HA HA HA HA HA HA HA HA HA HA HA HA HA HA HA HA HA HA HA HA HA HA HA HA HA HA HA HA HA HA

the end!

THE FEASTING STAR

Art by Lauren Henderso
Story by Sloane Leo

Sometimes it gives us back. That's what the humans want. For us to come back.

They're coming.
Easy now, they're just dressing you.

Hopefully we'll get some decent footage this time.
Tch, maybe, if she can outrun whatever's keeping them there.

You're fast, huh, Fern?

[The human call!]

[I need to seek something...]
beep!
beep!
beep!
[But what?]

[What could the humans want here?]

[Everything smells

...strange]

This couldn't be...

Food? Meat?

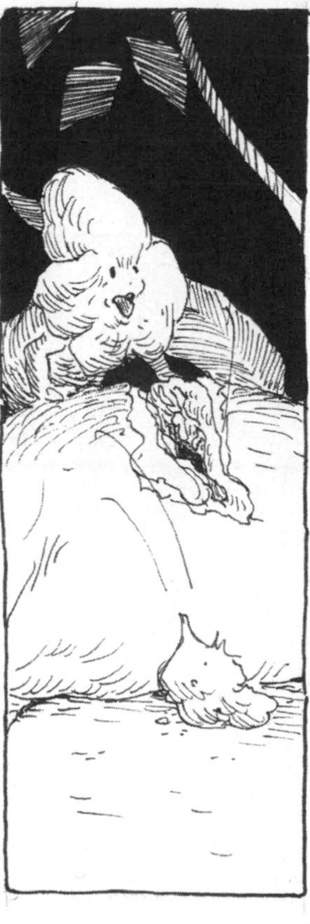

[These must be...pups!

And those are the older ones...
So there are families in this place as well.

SCREEECH

Sleep.

There!

Eat! Quickly!

Why is he like that? He's changed!

Yes yes. Changer of bodies.

Like stone to wind. Water to root.
Very powerful.

With me you shall come.
Be free of pale walkers.

Of stale blood and stubborn bone.
Be wind with me, small stranger...

...little gift.

[No...no!]

Be still now. Maybe he is quick with you.

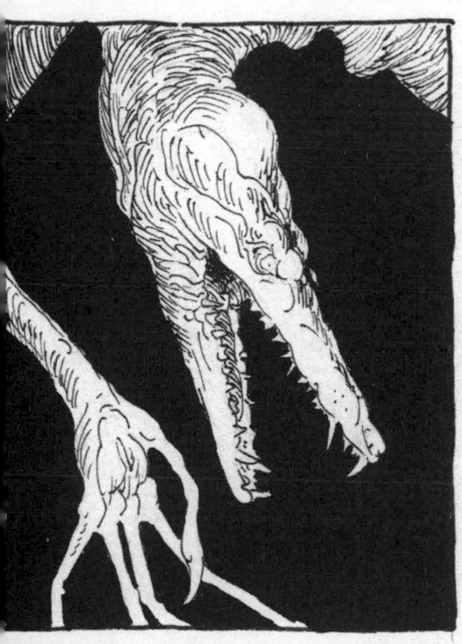

From afar, you come to me. I pray to *mothers, to* ancient nests, for strength. Then I see you, lightning *strike coat,* storm-eyed. You will bring me much strength, yes, *much* strength..
[Stop...*stop*]

[Please]

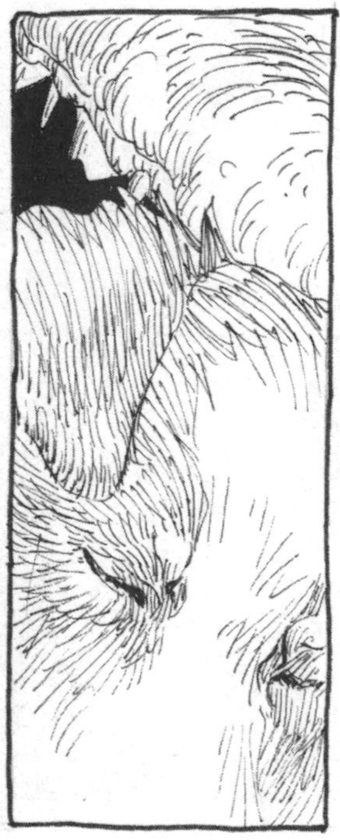

Jesus, it's Fern! She made it!

Quick, get some oxygen and the hazsuit.

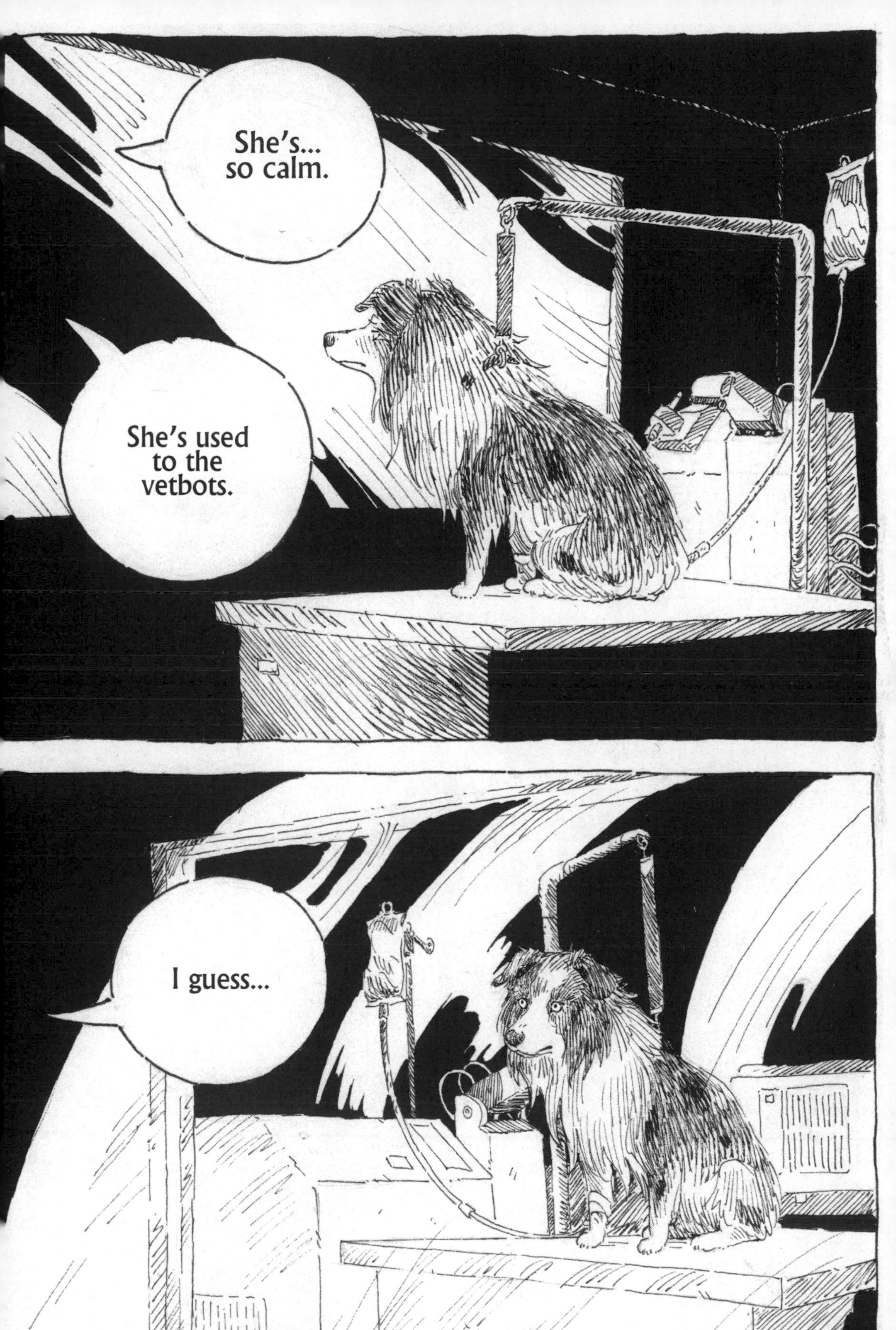
She's...
so calm.
She's used
to the
vetbots.
I guess...

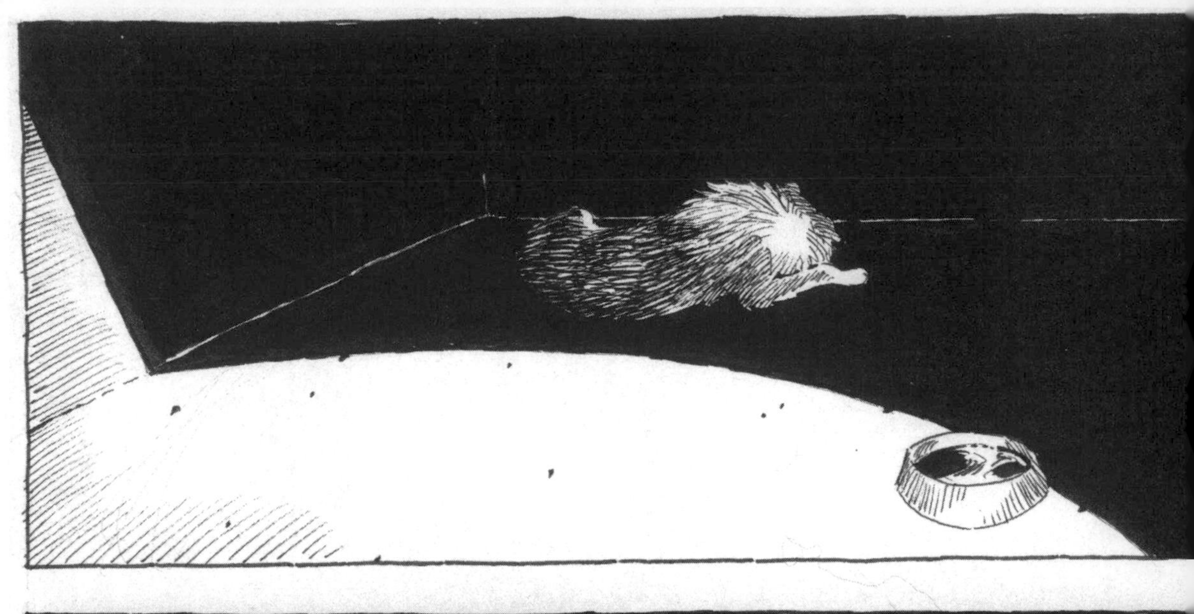

Come on girl, your quarantine is over; let's go see your friends!

I knew you'd be back! That's my girl!
What was it like? You smell so... weird.
The blue lands will do that to ya. That's what happened to Bailey.

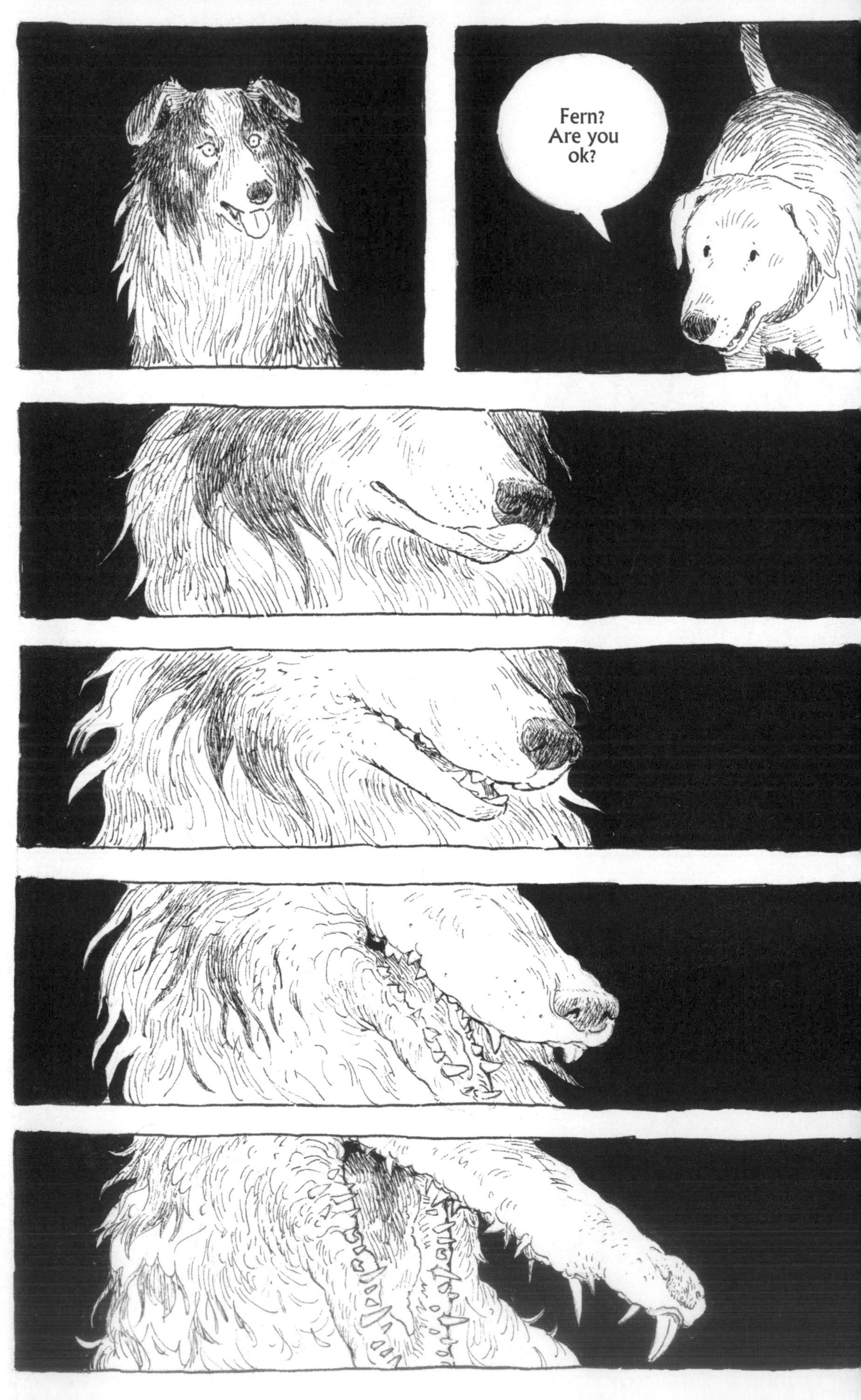
Fern?
Are you
ok?

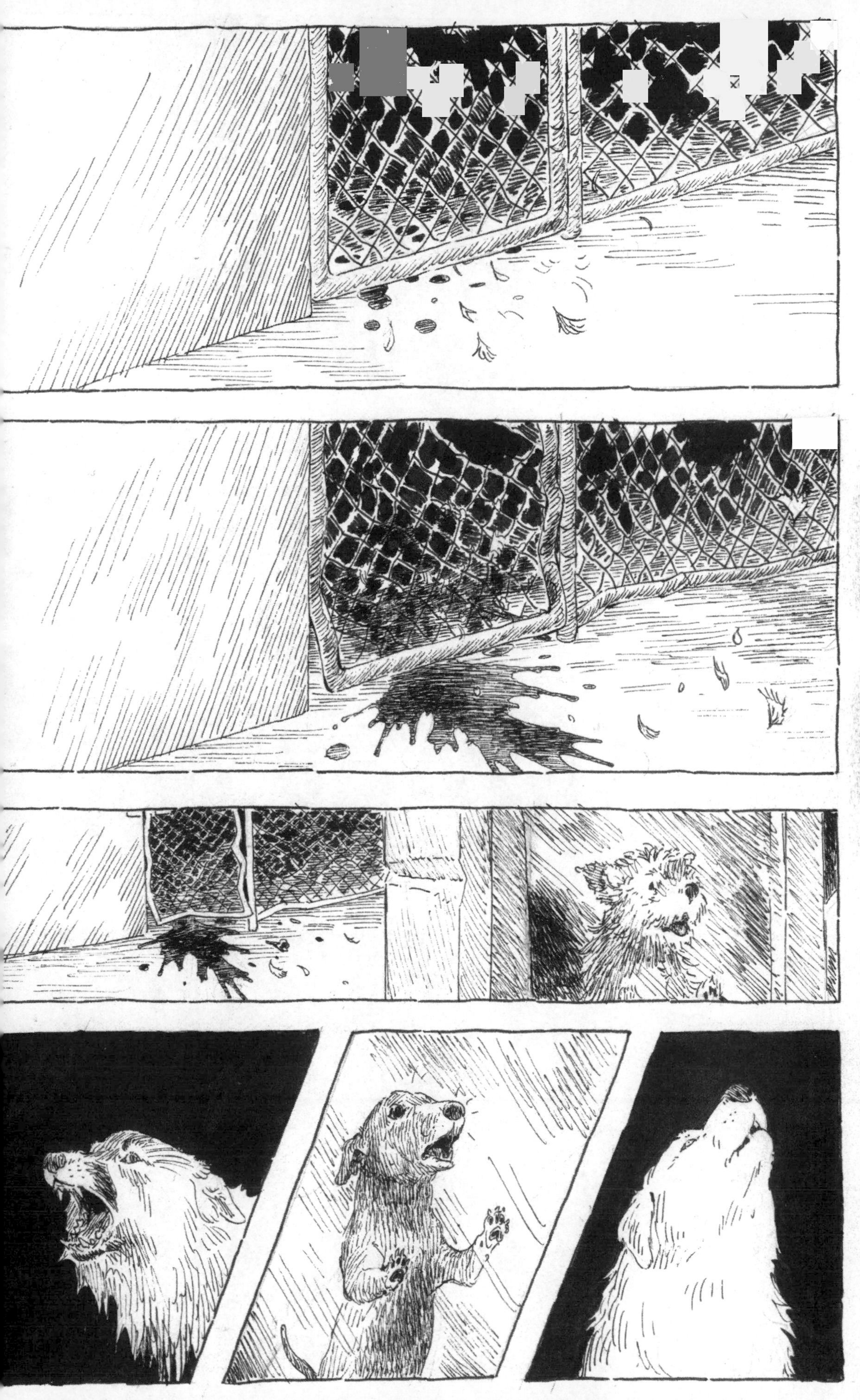

Lost and Found

Sam Davies

The Silk Crown
By:
Kanesha C. Bryant
I looked everywhere for Sis after the letters stopped.
Everywhere except Blue Rock, and then I looked there too.
Because when you have 100 siblings, you miss the one
that remembers your name.
Then the storm drove me
into the burrow...
...and the voices
led me deeper.

No one lives at Blue Rock.
I don't really remember my first steps into The Courtyard.

It was like
floating forward.
Pulled into the golden crowd
of strange bugs.

The Cicada were eager to welcome me. Never saw one outside of Mama's books, the last Emergence being so long ago. So I honestly thought they just...

I danced. And I know it's hard to believe that I didn't know something was wrong, but that place did something to me.
It put a feeling inside me that I think was supposed to be joy, but felt more like a wound healing too quickly.
And it made it hard to think, to speak, but I still asked about her. They told me she was there. My other questions went unanswered.
Questions weren't important anymore. She wasn't important anymore.
They asked me to stay and dance and I thought, maybe they're right.
Maybe she's not so important.
Asa...

I'd like to say the trance broke with the power of love, but really I was just angry. Angry that they almost made me forget her. Angry at myself for almost forgetting.

Angry enough to see the web.

I don't think they expected me to see it. Or at least, they didn't expect it to matter if I did.
I figured it was like any web though. They wanted me to struggle.
They wanted me to tangle myself up until I was still enough to hollow out.
So instead I calmed myself.
And I walked that web.
Until I found the edge.

And at the the edge
the web, I found her

And when I found her,
I pretended it wasn't
too late.

We talked for too long. I wanted to leave.

I held her paw and felt a desperate need to yank her forward,

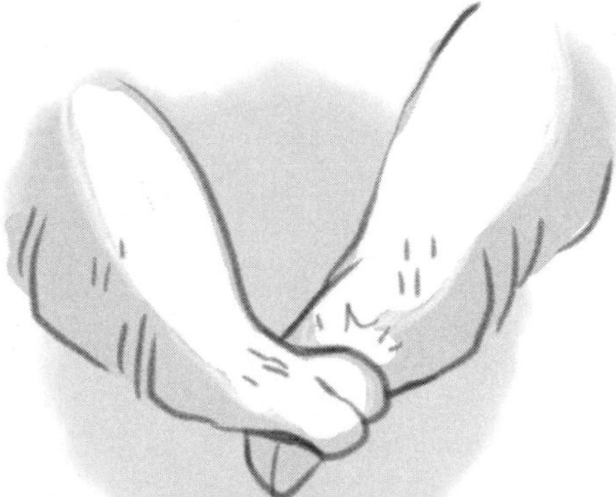

to pull and run and never stop until we were back home.

But I knew if I pulled she'd just...

She walked me to the middle of the courtyard, and I was glad because I don't think I could have left that room alone. I'm surprised she could leave at all with her legs just barely working.

She wasn't gone.

But she was going.

I thanked Anansi for every step.

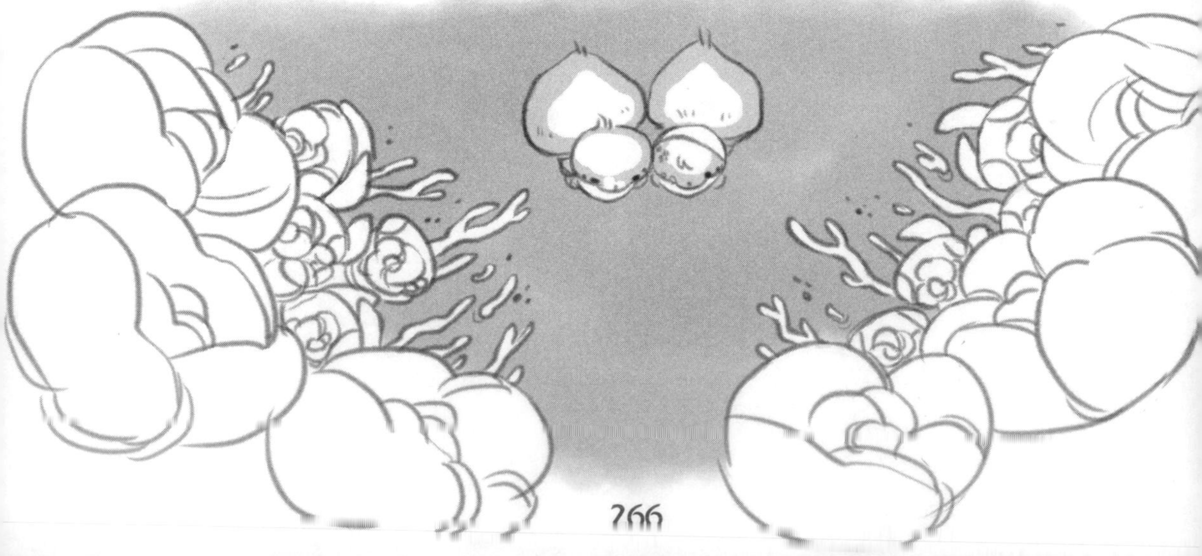

The longer she held out,
the longer I could pretend...

I could pretend we were both leaving.

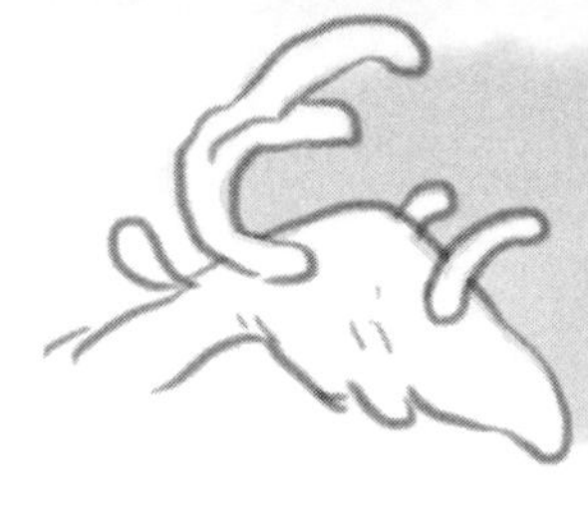

I was almost out before They Knew.

I had to run.

I didn't stop running for a long long time.

I didn't expect anyone to listen to me.
They never did before.
But everyone knows strange things happen at Blue Rock.

When they found the burrow, now nothing more than a clogged mess of those flowering...things in a tunnel that led nowhere, they looked to the holes.

When they found what was left of the cicada nymphs, tiny bodies missing heads and golden skins, they tried to burn what they could.

It didn't catch.
You can't fight Blue Rock.

I'm just glad I got to see her.
Before.
But I miss having someone who remembers my name.
Asa

a TAIL of TROUBLE
by ash g.
do y'think wickett's home?
of course, she hasn't left for months now.
that's what worries me.
KNOK KNOK
KNOK KNOK KNOK

oi! wick! it's me!
an' aggie!
CRASH
K-LUNK
SHUFFLE
SHUFFLE
??
!?!
oh!?
b-back already?
it didn't feel that long ago...
then again...
time seems to escape me lately.
aye, we didn't get lost this time!
took only a fortnight t'get to the fortess!
those wraiths gave us trouble without your magicks!
how goes recovery?

it's...g-going as well as it can go.
these things take time, as they say.
cooked up any new spells, lately?
umm.
no. n-not really, actually.
i've been...a bit preoccupied ...with -
oh?!
studying a new enchanted artifact?
let us see, wicky!
we've picked up another fer you as well!
i - i wasn't expecting guests so soon -
guest?!
we're family!
f-flik!
d-don't mind-

...mess.
MESS?!
wicky, this is a disa-
SHE'S NOT DAFT FLIK!
what happened?
jus' started with a harmless li'l grub.
each morn', there'd be another.
before i knew it, there were too many.
i jus'... couldn't.

aw... dear, you needn't do this alone.
i really did, mean to tell you, aggie.
but why trouble you with such small things?
there is no trouble too small, wicky.
the world can wait if a friend is in need.
aye, lean on us when y'need it.
sorry, for not asking for help, aggie.
nothin' to apologize fer.
what's important is that we can help now.
bet you could use something like THIS!

a wand? for me?
i-i haven't conjured a proper spell since the accident.
s'not like we can use it.
well, it doesn't need t'be a "proper" spell.
any spell should do, i think.
yer the most capable witch this side bramblewillow, after all.
even if we didn't say so!
i-i'll give it a go.

QUICK! now's our chance!

thank you
for everything.
knew y'had it in ya, wicky.
no grub can escape the powerful wickett of bramblew–
oh wait, no, there's one.
that one escaped.

guess i'll settle for "the sort-of-powerful wickett" in the meantime.
besides, they are still very cute.
in moderation, of course.
end.

PESTS

story by C. Spike Trotman
art by Amanda Lafrenais

oh my god

oh my GOD

oh MY god

oh
oh no
oh oh
rustl.
OH

Ah. Phew.
Miz Rory?
What are YOU doing here?
Are you okay?

H
H-hey, Russ! You oughta be asleep, kiddo!
Is it a dog?

I can bite him.
Ha ha, no, it's good. Y'know, I just-
there was a sound. Got a li'l spooked! Ha ha!

HA ha HA HA!
Oh-KAY, back to bed!
Hey, have you seen my DAD?
Uh.
... yes?
Is he coming? I'm hungry.
POK
Yiiiiiiiiii!!
Lou-!
YIP YIP YIP YIP YIP!
Don't let him-
He won't get far.

WUMPH
See?
COME ON.
This way.
THUMP
Oh!
Ha. Didn't even see it.
Yeah. Never gets old, huh?
CRAK
crunch

OKay, uh. Hey, so, Russ, your dad's told you about people, right?
How sometimes-
Skin apes.
Oh-Kay, well, don't call them *that*, but.
Y'y'Know how- sometimes people just- they do mean stuff to us? Not to eat, just to.
Do it?
Yeah.
W-well, a uh. A mean thing happened to your dad, tonight. And it's nothing he did, oKay? And nothing you did.
I Know.
Right, good. And, uhm.
Miss Rory is gonna.
Look after you for a little bit, oKay? She'll sleep here in the den and bring you meals. Cuz.
Cuz dad isn't coming back tonight.
OKay.

"Okay?"
Yeah. I'm not a baby.
... oh.
When IS he coming back?

aurora
aurora you got thumbs right
604
604
LOU!!

LOUIS, OH MY GOD, ARE YOU OKAY
LOU WHAT HAPPENED
NO
I DON'T KNOW I got a bee sting and I went to sleep and I got stuck GET IT OFF
Oh jeez, oh wow, I don't know if I can-
DAD!
DAD?
DAD YOU'RE A DOG?!
WHAT?? WHAT DID YOU TELL HIM?
Are you serious I thought you were DEAD I couldn't tell him ANYTHING
SKIN APES
HEY
NO!
Oooooh, my god.
I'm so glad I do not have to raise your terrible child.
My kid is amazing please help me
Yeah I definitely can't.
END

CREATORS

Abby Howard is a Boston-based cartoonist who creates the webcomics *Junior Scientist Power Hour* and *The Last Halloween*. She also published an educational graphic novel with Abrams Books, *Earth Before Us: Dinosaur Empire*. She loves dinosaurs and spooky tales, and has a very cute cat.

Aliza Layne contains four cleptoparasitic genera of bees that oviposit their eggs onto or near the pollen stores of their hosts' nests. These bees are host generalists and belong to a lineage of parasites that uniquely shares no specificity with any nonparasitic halictine taxa. More comics at alizalayne.com.

Amanda Lafrenais is an independent, self-taught comics artist. Born in Humble, Texas, she now lives in Clute—home to the Mosquito Festival. Yes. She is the creator of the popular webcomic *Love Me Nice*, and a regular contributor to both the Slipshine erotic comics site and Iron Circus Comics' *Smut Peddler* anthology series.

Ana Sabater is a comic artist and illustrator who has mostly worked in small press and self-publishing projects, like her latest block print comic *Olvido*. Currently living in between Belgium and Spain, and juggling animation studies on top of it, she tries to keep on creating stories while feeding her old hungry black cat. She loves him but she is allergic to cats, which may be kind of a life metaphor.

Anna Wieszczyk is a comic artist and illustrator living in Krakow, Poland.
annawieszczyk.deviantart.com

Ash G. enlisted in the U.S. Navy on the promise of endless waves of big, beefy dudes as far as the eye could see. She draws comics to cope with the disappointing reality of the situation until she discovers where Godzilla is sleeping in the depths of the ocean.
kilo-monster.com

C. Spike Trotman is a cartoonist and publisher who was born in DC, raised in MD, and currently resides in Chicago, IL. She likes anchovies, roughhousin' dogs, and god games. Iron Circus Comics belongs to her, but she'll let you hold it if you ask nicely.
ironcircus.com

Claudia Cangini is a freelance illustrator and comic artist living in Italy. She mainly draws for RPGs and comics, and loves sneakily subverting visual and narrative tropes.

claudiacangini.deviantart.com

David McGuire is a medium-sized omnivorous mammal who has been considering becoming a pescatarian but hasn't yet taken the plunge.

Eli Church is a bright, shiny skeleton in a greasy, terrible shell. They live in Vancouver, British Columbia.

medium.com/@Preapocalypse

Evan Dahm has been creating and self-publishing graphic novels since 2006, including *Rice Boy*, *Order of Tales*, and *Vattu*. He is from North Carolina and lives in New York.

Gavin Falcon is a comic author based out of St. Louis, Missouri; spending much of his time behind the counter at his business, NewCastle Comics and Games. His recent Google search history includes "How to write a short bio for comics".

Graham Overby is a graduate of the Sequential Art program at the Savannah College of Art and Design, class of 2014. He hails from Falls Church, Virginia, just south of DC, and currently resides in Philly. Growing up, his best friend's family had a basset hound named Sebastian who was silly and loving and stubborn as a mule. You can find more of Graham's comics and illustration work at grahamoverby.tumblr.com.

Jemma Salume is a comic artist and illustrator. She has created comics and zines such as *Overreact*, *Avenge*, and *Thief/Fighter/Witch*. She has also done covers for *Smut Peddler* and Boom Studios, and comics for *Mouse Guard*, Ryan Estrada's *Broken Telephone*, and various anthologies. She lives and works in Portland, Oregon, and is determined to be friends with every cat in the city.

Jessi Zabarsky is a cartoonist and illustrator living in Chicago. She makes stories about very small spaces and moments in very big worlds. She likes bunnies, plants, and snacks. Jessi was raised in the woods and will someday return there.

Kanesha C. Bryant discovered that books can both lead you into magical worlds of wonder and rip your heart in two like a cheap paper towel at a very young age. She then learned to write and draw her own stories, so she could turn this terrible power on others. She loves monsters, horror stories, and learning cool facts about nature.

Down and out in Massachusetts, **KC Green** writes and draws comics for a long time, then a longer time happens where he is playing video games or watching the same five YouTube ASMR videos. The day starts again in much the same path, but instead maybe it's Wednesday and not Tuesday. kcgreendotcom.com

Lauren Henderson is a comic artist and illustrator living in Nashua, New Hampshire. guldentusks.tumblr.com

Lindsey Lea is an animator and designer at ShadowMachine. Loves dogs, tofu, and Polaroids. grumble-bee.tumblr.com

Natalie Riess is a eusocial insect of the family Formicidae and, along with the related wasps and bees, belongs to the order Hymenoptera. She is easily identified by her elbowed antennae and the distinctive node-like structure that forms her slender waist. Comics and illustration at natalieriess.com.

Rachel Dukes is a cartoonist, cat enthusiast, and co-host of the podcast *The Ink Pit.* She is thankful for coffee, gingham, and readers like you.
mixtapecomics.com

Ryan Estrada is an artist/adventurer who lives in Busan, South Korea. He was once thrown from a train in India. He slept on two different Japanese park benches in two different typhoons. He was almost eaten by lions in Kenya. He was arrested in Ecuador. His work can be found at ryanestrada.com. One of those things is a lie.

Sam Davies makes the all-ages silent webcomic *Stutterhug* and the long form series *The Shape of Things*—both of which regularly feature small creatures in peril, though usually only from their own feelings. *The Wind in The Willows* was a special favourite as a kid, so her story here features a little moley of her own in tribute. She's based in the UK, which has all the cold weather, ugly dogs and ghost stories she could wish for.
stutterhug.tumblr.com
tapas.io/series/Stutterhug

Sarah O'Donnell is 5'2" half-Japanese, half-Polish/Irish/Lithuanian "windup doll" (according to an art teacher she had once). She lives in Tokyo with a boy with glasses and two unrelated tuxedo cats. She draws comics, makes websites, hosts podcasts, and takes pictures. She also spends too much time thinking about money, food and human behavior. Her favorite pastime is drinking too much and watching copious amounts of Guy Fieri.
forfoxsake.org

Sloane Leong is a self-taught cartoonist, artist and writer currently living in Portland, Oregon and has done work for Image Comics, Cartoon Network, DC, and more. She's currently working on a girls' basketball YA graphic novel called *A Map to the Sun* for First Second.

Will Strode writes and draws! He also storyboards at ShadowMachine!
grizzlywilliam.tumblr.com